"Aye, it's you, Slocum," Simon Bergereon said with a sardonic grin. The rest of his men on horseback formed a semicircle. The titter of their anxious laughter caused a cold chill to run up Slocum's spine.

"What's your business here?" Slocum asked.

"Oh, we've got business, Slocum. Lots of business. Where's your partner?" Bergereon looked around. . . .

Slocum let the man's words shed off like so much rain, but inside, a rising fire of anger knotted him up. "Whatever you got in mind, Bergereon, get on with it. But I'll guarantee you'll be the one that dies here."

"Brave words for a man way outnumbered."

"Numbers don't count. It's who dies first. Were you in the war?"

"Yes." Bergereon's dark eyes narrowed as he drew up the reins to settle his horse.

"Then you've seen men die all kinds of ways. Only thing, a bullet never found *you*."

"That's right. What're you getting at?"

"Death. Yours . . ."

DON'T MISS THESE
ALL-ACTION WESTERN SERIES
FROM THE BERKLEY PUBLISHING GROUP

THE GUNSMITH by J. R. Roberts
> Clint Adams was a legend among lawmen, outlaws, and ladies. They called him . . . the Gunsmith.

LONGARM by Tabor Evans
> The popular long-running series about U.S. Deputy Marshal Long—his life, his loves, his fight for justice.

SLOCUM by Jake Logan
> Today's longest-running action Western. John Slocum rides a deadly trail of hot blood and cold steel.

BUSHWHACKERS by B. J. Lanagan
> An action-packed series by the creators of Longarm! The rousing adventures of the most brutal gang of cutthroats ever assembled—Quantrill's Raiders.

JAKE LOGAN

SLOCUM AND THE BUFFALO HUNTER

J

JOVE BOOKS, NEW YORK

SLOCUM AND THE BUFFALO HUNTER

A Jove Book / published by arrangement with
the author

PRINTING HISTORY
Jove edition / June 1999

The Penguin Putnam Inc. World Wide Web site address is
http://www.penguinputnam.com

ISBN: 0-515-12518-0

A JOVE BOOK®
Jove Books are published by The Berkley Publishing Group,
a division of Penguin Putnam Inc.,
375 Hudson Street, New York, New York 10014.
JOVE and the "J" design
are trademarks belonging to Penguin Putnam Inc.

PRINTED IN THE UNITED STATES OF AMERICA

10 9 8 7 6 5 4 3 2 1

SLOCUM AND
THE BUFFALO HUNTER

1

He turned his collar to the wind. If this cold kept on, it surely would snow. Just their luck. Low blue clouds hung close enough to the ground that a man on horseback would think he could reach up and touch them. He rose in the saddle and looked back over the herd of horses that followed the noisy bell tied under his gray mare's throat. The eternal clanging of the clapper had become little more than background noise after six weeks on the trail north. Shorty Bob Giles looked half asleep in the saddle, bringing up the rear of the herd and leading the two packhorses. Not much work to driving broken horses; these geldings would follow the gray mare Slocum rode to hell and back.

Weather niggled him. He knew they'd left Texas way too late to ever reach Nebraska before winterlike conditions set in. His greatest concern was getting back out of there before things were locked up tight in snow and ice. Still, work was work, and Jim Brady had sold these ranch horses to a man named McBroom outside of Ogallala. Brady had hired Slocum and Giles to deliver them to the MC Ranch. All Slocum could think about was the fact it was a long way from San Antonio and its warm, sunny plazas. With a gut-churning longing, Slocum recalled the inviting sway of the pretty *señoritas'* shapely hips at the cantinas. Next time, he wouldn't be so anxious to sign on. Besides, Jim Brady had never done an honest day's work in his entire life; he made deals and hired others to do the labor.

Something flickered in the corner of his eye. Slocum tried to look off across the dark waving sea of eternal grass and find what he had noticed. But he saw nothing as he carefully checked the eastern horizon.

"Shorty, get up here and ride this mare," he shouted. Despite the fact that he saw nothing, something out there had made the hair on the back of his neck stand up. He stepped off the mare and undid the left stirrup. Wary the entire time, he kept checking the rise for any other signs while he worked to undo the stirrup lacing. Quickly, he shortened the fender two notches, and then went to the other side of the mare and did the same.

"What's happening?" Shorty asked, reining up and stepping off his bay.

"We've got company out there. You take Eagle here and the horse herd. Keep that Winchester of yours real close." He squinted to better check the horizon. Not a thing in sight. He took the right side and Shorty took the left, and they hastily lengthened the stirrups on Shorty's saddle.

"You speaking of Injun company?" Shorty narrowed his eyes with serious concern.

"Yes. I'm sure I saw a white feather sticking up out of the corner of my eye."

"Damn devils. We knew if they ever saw this herd we would be dead men." He handed the reins to the bay to Slocum, and then Shorty climbed on the gray mare. His efforts rang the clapper under her throat and as if on cue, the horses' heads came up from grazing, ready to move on with her.

"Do we need to break and run for it?" Shorty asked.

"No. That way they'd pick off part of the herd. Can't be over four or five of them out there looking for some horseflesh to steal."

"And we've got fifty of them." Shorty leaned back and jerked the long gun out of the scabbard. "Guess this is what is called earning your keep."

"Yeah. Keep you eyes peeled."

"Hey, you be careful, hear me?"

"I will. It's my hair." Slocum reined the big bay around. He was a powerful animal with great legs, and they called him Bugger. He could outdistance most horses from a jump start in three lengths. According to his previous owner, Bugger could scent Indians at a mile. He hated Redskins, and Slocum planned to depend on the big horse to tell him what he could not see. On the first rise, Slocum made a wide swing east to see if he could flush out the spy or an outrider.

The bay wanted to run, so he let him. The wind whistled past Slocum's face as he rode low in the saddle, hoping to make a smaller target. Sun-cured grass parted and when he reached the hilltop, he reined in the bay. Bugger danced around on his front feet as Slocum held him back and blinked in disbelief at the sight before him.

Three women with dogs were hurrying across the prairie ahead. One squaw had a papoose on her back. They looked back at him with wary dark eyes, and then they trotted faster to the north. The three dogs carried light travois loads. One woman wore a single eagle feather, and it had been her that he had seen spying on him. There were no men in sight, which struck him as peculiar as he considered it. Better see what he could learn about the women. He stood up in the stirrups and set off in a long trot to catch them.

At the sight of him coming toward them, they looked at each other in shock and then began to run. Black braids flew, copper calves flashed, and buckskin fringes danced in the wind. The oldest woman whipped the dogs with a willow switch to make them hurry; they yelped in pain each time she struck them. Tails tucked under their butts, they made the travois sticks sing on the grass.

"Wait!" Slocum shouted. "I am a friend!" He opened the bay up into a gallop, swung him wide around the fleeing women, and then circled back at them. Drawing in the reins, he stopped the big horse in the path of their flight and faced them. He held his hand up in the sign of peace; then he advanced toward them.

Bugger snorted and slung his head. Slocum almost grinned at the bay's reaction to the women. He surely didn't like Indians. A horse like that was invaluable when a man's life depended on it. Slocum spoke softly to reassure him. The bay calmed some, but not without blowing some fierce snorts out of the rollers in his nose.

"Good day," he said to the women with a nod as the bay danced around under him. "Where are you going?"

One of the women said something in Sioux, and it made no sense to Slocum.

The youngest one bore the papoose. In her teens, she was the plain-looking one of the three. Nose too big, lips too thick, and her eyes were slanted like an Oriental's. The oldest woman carried lots of gray in her hair, parted in the middle and pulled so tight in braids that her eyes were slits. Her mouth was fractured with a million sun wrinkles. But her eyes were sharp as hard coal and she watched him closely.

The third said her name was One Feather, and she stood tall for an Indian woman, perhaps five eight. Her ripe breasts pushed out the pumpkin-colored leather blouse. The leather skirt clung to her narrow hips. Her hair was in braids wrapped in rabbit fur. Small colorful feathers decorated the braids, and they fluttered in the wind.

"What do you want?" One Feather demanded in English as if inconvenienced by his stopping them.

"What do *you* want?" Slocum asked, grasping the saddle-horn and looking close at her handsome face. "You spied on me first."

"To be left alone," she said. In defiant pride, she took a stance in front of the other two.

"Do you have any food for that baby?" He nodded toward it, wondering what they had to eat.

"He is not yours to worry about," One Feather insisted as if she were shielding the baby from him.

"I have some canned milk, if he needs it," Slocum said.

"For what price?" she asked, sticking her breasts out when she jerked her shoulders square. He didn't miss how the breasts firmly quaked under the buckskin.

"Nothing if he needs it," he said, and shook his head to dismiss her concern, though mentally he was tempted to say she could have the milk for a favor from her.

The three women talked in guttural voices with each other,

casting wary looks at him as he dismounted and squatted on his boot heels beside the bay. They obviously were undecided about his gift. At last, they agreed with nods and One Feather stepped toward him, but still kept her distance.

"We accept your offer. Sell us a horse," she said quickly.

He blinked at her. "They aren't my horses to sell. They belong to another man."

"We would take a small one."

"One horse?" He looked at her with a wry set to his mouth as he considered her request. One horse and three women, what good would that do? "Why one horse?"

"Our dogs are tired. We have little to feed them. We could let the horse carry our things and the papoose."

"How much would you pay for a horse?" he asked, slapping the reins on his leg as he shifted his weight to his other foot and considered the sale of one horse. So they'd be short one pony when they got to McBroom. Brady had sent some extras. Back in Texas they had lost a horse to a rattlesnake bite. Might be time to lose another.

"Where are you going?" he asked to satisfy his curiosity.

"To join our people."

"Where are they?"

"That way," she said with the same vagueness as before. Then the oldest woman said a few Sioux words. "We can pay you twenty dollars," One Feather added.

"You have twenty dollars?" he asked, shaken by the fact she might not be lying to him.

"Yes," she said, digging in her leather pouch and then holding out her hand with two small ten-dollar gold pieces that shone despite the poor light. She had the longest fingers he could ever recall, slender but long. Her fist closed on the money as she waited for his reply.

"One horse, some milk," he said to himself. He had no idea how far these women were going, but if Brady couldn't spare them one horse, it was too damn bad. "Do you have a rope?" he asked, and remounted.

"Yes," she said.

"Good," he said, and booted the bay back in the direction of the herd.

In a short while, he topped the ridge and saw the instant relief on Shorty's face at his return.

"I need one horse," he said, pushing the bay into the herd and looking for the mousy blue roan. The least horse in the whole herd, but enough for the women's needs.

"Get out four cans of milk too," he said to Shorty as he spotted the roan and shook loose his lariat.

"Four cans of condensed milk?"

"Yes," he said, and rose in the stirrups and threw the loop. It settled on the roan's head. He dallied it off around his horn, and the roan drew it tight and then settled down. Talking softly, he rode up close, fashioned a halter on the roan's head, and came out leading him.

"What are you doing with four cans of milk and a horse?" A mild look of amusement and wonder twinkled in Shorty's green eyes.

"Anyone ever asks, an Injun got this roan. That milk is a gift from you."

Shorty frowned. "To who?"

"Prettiest damn squaw I've seen in a while. You want to deliver it?"

"Naw, I'll let you, seeing as you're making the deal." A sly smile spread over Shorty's beard-stubbled face. "Slocum, any man that could find a good-looking woman clear out here—I don't know about." With a wary head shake, Shorty handed him the milk cans one at a time.

"It's all charity," Slocum said with a shrug, sticking them inside his coat pockets. "She offered me twenty for the horse."

"Twenty bucks for *him*?" Shorty reared back in disbelief. "If Brady gave five for him, he gave five too much."

"I figure the man getting these horses in Nebraska would only complain about the roan if he saw him."

"Probably. Where in the hell did an Injun squaw get twenty bucks? You give her that?" Shorty grinned from ear to ear at his notion.

"I don't know and she didn't say."

"What's she need milk for?"

"A baby. And it ain't hers."

"They all say that."

"You can come see for yourself," Slocum offered, and jerked the reluctant roan around on the lead as he prepared to leave his partner.

"Have fun," Shorty said, and waved him away. "Glad they ain't renegades."

The bay short-loped, and the smaller horse was forced to join him or be dragged. Slocum topped the rise, and could see the women looking back with their hands shielding their eyes against the weak sun. They still must be wondering why he was doing all this.

"Here is your horse," he said, and held out the lead rope for One Feather. She came up with a braided leather lariat, and spoke to the horse with authority. The roan snorted softly at her. Slocum could see she was no stranger to horses and took the roan over with authority. This woman knew how to handle horses. In an instant, she had her lead on the roan, and handed back Slocum's lariat.

"Here is your money," she said, and he shook his head.

"No, you keep it and buy more milk for the baby." He dismissed her offer with a wave of his hand. *Hell, ole Brady could spare her one horse.*

She nodded and turned to the roan. Her face close to his muzzle, she talked to him and stroked his nose with her hands, then breathed in his nostrils.

"What is your name?" Slocum asked, ready to pull out.

Her words were in Sioux, and he shook his head. He didn't savvy a single portion of it. No way he ever would.

"Feather." He indicated the eagle feather in her braid. "You are Feather to me."

"What is your name?" she asked, jutting her oval chin out with her words.

"Slocum."

She said it slowly as if she savored the word. "Someday I will repay you, Slo-cum."

"I will look forward to that day. Go in peace, Feather."

She nodded. He bobbed his head for her. The whole time they'd talked he'd considered her shapely body under the leather clothing. There was a lot of woman there, but she probably belonged to some scalp-hungry buck. Then forced to check Bugger, Slocum reined him around and rode over to give the oldest woman the cans of milk.

His business complete, he gave Feather a last look. She was busy packing the roan with their things. Thoughts of how she would look naked made his stomach roil. He drew a deep breath, and then he set spurs to Bugger.

Ain't going half bad up here, Brady, we're almost across Kansas. I guess you could afford losing one sorry horse. We've got the rest, and in a week should be at that ranch with them. As he hunched his shoulders to the cold, he could visualize Brady lounging in some sunny cantina with a fine *señorita* in his lap. *Cross your fingers, old boy, that all of our Injun encounters ain't any worse than that one.*

2

"Where're we camping tonight?" Shorty asked, riding up close to him in the late afternoon.

"I'd like to find a pen or corral, so we don't have to night-herd them for one night," Slocum said. He squinted hard to see better from under the shade of his hat brim, searching across the rolling brown grassland.

"That would be nice," Shorty agreed with a nod. "If Brady hadn't been so damn cheap, there should have been three of us, instead of two to share that night-hawking business."

"He'd only pay us less." Slocum laughed and dismissed the notion with a shrug. "We'll let them graze a while along here and I'll check out the country. There's bound to be several ranches around here. Someone should have a trap that we can put them in overnight."

"Good idea. You want to switch horses?" Shorty indicated the gray mare he rode.

"No, I'll cut that big bay with the white snip in his face to ride. He looks stout enough. We'll let Bugger here and the mare get some grass this afternoon."

A sly grin on his lips, Shorty looked undecided over his choice of horseflesh. "You might have you a little excitement too. That bay's got lots of white around his old eyes when he gets riled up."

Slocum wiped his mouth on his palm, then with his thumb rubbed away the fine grit from the corners. A good hot bath would surely go just fine at the moment. He shook down his lariat as he rode along, considering the big mahogany-colored horse, and decided Snip might just bog his head a little if a man tried to ride him.

No time like the present to find out. He worked the loop larger, swung it twice, and reached out. Snip's head punched a hole in it and Slocum jerked the slack. At his capture, the pony snorted and threw his ears up as if awakened from a soft dream. Slocum tied off his rope on the saddlehorn. Other than his wide-eyed look, Snip gave little fight at being caught. Obviously he was rope-broke.

Slocum stepped off Bugger and went down the lariat. The horse trembled at his touch, but soon settled, and Slocum led him up close to change the saddle over to his back. When Snip was at last rigged and the bridle in place, Slocum turned Bugger loose and then coiled up his rope. The horse herd had taken the opportunity to drop their heads and graze. Shorty leaned on his horn of his saddle with a look of anticipation and ready to watch the show.

Slocum held the bridle cheek strap close to his knee when he mounted. Snip circled anxiously under him as he swung his leg over and took a seat aboard him. When he released the hold, the pony swallowed his head and exploded. With stiff-legged crow-hops, he went out through the others, scattering the herd. His effort gave Slocum's riding skills a good enough test, but nothing to worry about. Slocum began to saw on the bits, and tried to jerk Snip's head off. That only served to encourage the big horse. He did a sunfish up in the sky, where Slocum felt certain that the weak sun shone right on the girth under the horse's belly.

He could hear Shorty hollering in the distance. "Ride him, cowboy! Ride him!"

Enough was enough. If Snip wanted to buck, Slocum decided to make him do it until his tongue hung out. Slocum went to slashing him from side to side with the reins and spurring him up and down his sides.

Snip gave a squeal like a pig caught under a gate, and

decided that by running away he might escape the punishment. In a burst of speed, he tore away across the prairie. Slocum soon had him under control, and then short-loped him back to where Shorty sat on his horse, laughing at him.

"Damn, he's a stout sumbitch," Shorty said with a rueful shake of his head. "Old Man Ames use to say he wouldn't keep a horse didn't have some buck in him. He'd sure like that bay devil"

"I'll go ride some of that out of him," Slocum said, and reined the horse around. Snip's training came back swiftly, and he began to act like a using horse with his nonsense over. Slocum left Shorty to watch the herd, and rode north looking for a place to lock the herd up for the night.

A few miles on, he spotted a low-walled sod house, and he headed toward it. They had a good size-lodgepole pen, and Slocum hoped he and Shorty could use it. Neither he nor Shorty had had a full night's sleep in over five weeks.

A bareheaded man came out of the house. The wind mussed his thin hair and he flattened it with his hand. He had his galluses down and wore a faded underwear top, and his canvas pants were tucked into high-top boots. He looked around forty years old, with some gray in his beard.

"Howdy," Slocum offered.

"Howdy yourself, stranger."

"Slocum's my name," he said, looking around. The pens looked plenty big enough to hold the herd, and he felt that he might have found a good place.

"Henry Alderson," the man said. "Climb down. What can I do for you?"

"This your place, Henry?"

"Yep, I buy hides, do some trading. Guess you can see the stacks of them out back there. You got any to sell?"

"No, we're trailing a herd of horses up to Ogallala and wondered if we could use your pens tonight to hold them."

"Make yourself at home. I ain't expecting no one to need them."

"Much obliged. We'll drive them up slow so they get a good fill of grass, and then spend the night here. Be glad to pay you."

"No need. But I've got store goods and some whiskey for sale if you need it."

"I'm sure Shorty and I'll want to sample some." He saluted the man and set Snip into a long lope.

Over the past weeks, he'd seen several antelope and some black-tail deer. But that much meat would spoil, hot as the days had been in the past before they could eat it, so he'd allowed them to disappear. It wouldn't be long until they were at the McBroom ranch anyway, and a big outfit like that usually served good ranch chuck for folks like him and Shorty delivering horses to them.

He caught up with Shorty on a rise. The horses were spread out over a wide area, heads down grazing.

"Found a store and a pen up ahead where we can corral them. I'll catch the gray mare and lead her. We'll take our time driving them up there."

"Ah, yes. Thank the Lord for a pen," Shorty said gratefully. "I'll sure enjoy some peaceful sleep tonight for a change."

Slocum agreed, and set Snip after the gray mare. With his rope on her neck and the bell clanging under her throat, the horses picked up their heads as if on cue and began to ramble after her. Slocum looked back as Shorty pushed the stragglers up.

Slocum led them to a moon lake, one of the many fresh-water ponds on the prairie that had no outlets in a basin that filled with the melting snow and rainfall. These ponds shrank and expanded with the dry-wet cycles. Lucky for him and Shorty, this year they were still half-full in the early fall. Some pintail ducks rose at their approach, then in a short while returned and lighted on the water, quacking, satisfied the herd was no threat. The sound of horses pawing, splashing, and drinking, mingled with the ducks' quacking, carried to Slocum's ears as he squatted on his boot heels, grateful that the day was about over.

He watched the horses stomp and toss water on their backs. Satisfied they'd had enough to drink, he remounted and led the mare off. The bell clanged under her throat latch. The reluctant horses came with a little help from Shorty, and they were soon lined out for Alderson's store.

When at last Slocum swung the gate shut on them, the sun dropped to a point flat with the horizon. Slocum nodded his approval, and Alderson came down to look them over.

"Nice set of horses. Who gets them?" Alderson asked.

"McBroom ranch," Shorty said as he and Slocum unsaddled.

"Why, you aren't two days' ride from there," Alderson said.

"Good. Is it a big outfit?" Shorty asked.

"No. In fact, I can't figure out why him and her need fifty horses, but maybe he's going to sell part of them or make a cattle drive."

"Don't make a damn to me what he does with them," Shorty said. "They're going to be his worry in how many days?"

"Two days, easy riding."

"You hear that, Slocum?"

"I did," Slocum said, setting the first pannier from the packhorses on the ground. "I didn't tell Shorty yet that you had whiskey for sale."

"He does?" Shorty about choked on his words.

"I sure do," Alderson said. "Come on up after you get settled."

"We'll be up there very shortly."

The packhorses were rubbed down. Then they and the saddle horses were turned in with the herd. Slocum and Shorty headed for the store. They used the pitcher and basin the man set out for them on the table outside, and washed up. Slocum felt pleased to have his gritty face clean for the first time in days as he dried himself on the sack towel.

"What's that noise?" Shorty asked with a frown.

"Mules," Alderson said, coming out the front door. "Must be Burgereon coming in."

"Who?" Shorty asked as the three of them went to see the spectacle.

"Simon Bergereon, a big buffalo hunter, and his outfit of skinners and shooters."

"Is he going to need the corral?" Slocum asked. He could see the long line of noisy jackasses under their packs in the blood path of the sunset. A tall figure cradling a rifle came in the lead. He was dressed in buckskin, and the wind whipped the long fringe on his sleeves as the stalwart man approached. Several riders rode up and down the line, whacking mules with quirts to get them in line.

Alderson dismissed Slocum's concern. "You were here first," he said.

"He sell you his hides?" Shorty asked.

Alderson shook his head. "He's too big a deal for that. He takes his directly to the Choteau brothers. That's why I didn't ask you to move your horses."

"Who sells you hides then?" Shorty asked under his breath.

"Injuns, small outfits, some settlers shoot a few, bring me the hides. No, Simon is too big a man to deal with me."

"Alderson," Bergereon said, and tossed his leg over the saddlehorn and then lighted on his moccasins. "Gentlemen." He gave Slocum and Shorty a nod.

"How's the hunting?" Alderson asked.

"Disgustingly good. I see the corrals are full." He rose on the toes of his knee-high moccasins and viewed the horse herd with a wry set to his mouth.

"Yes, they are," Alderson said. "Slocum and Shorty, meet Simon Bergereon."

"Whose horses?" the man asked, as if Slocum and Shorty did not exist, still looking over the herd.

"McBroom ranch ordered them," Slocum said, not impressed with this man, who obviously considered himself some sort of royalty of the plains.

"Oh, well, then drive them out and we'll put our mules in there."

Slocum shook his head for Alderson to stay back. He stepped up to the man. "I see you have plenty of gear on those mules, mister."

"I do." His dark eyes filled with suspicion, and he looked Slocum over from head to foot.

"You got a shovel in all that stuff?"

"Certainly. Why?"

"I'm glad you got one, because if you open that gate and turn out those horses, I'll need it to plant you with. Do I make myself clear?"

"Slocum, huh?" His gaze turned icy. "I won't forget that either."

"You can carve it on your tombstone. Don't mess with those horses."

"Obviously we will have to hobble our mules, Randolph," Bergereon said over his shoulder to his man as he rode up. "Mr. Slocum here has the corrals reserved."

"Reserved!" the man shouted in disbelief.

"Hobble the gawdamn mules, Randolph."

Satisfied that their possession of the corrals was settled, Slocum ducked his head and went inside the post. Those buffalo hunters would bear watching. They were a tough lot, and he knew they weren't fools either.

Alderson's buffalo stew beat Slocum and Shorty's cooking, and the two of them ate a second large bowl of it seated at table by themselves. The hide hunters had filed in, and were lined at the raw-board bar, downing wildcat whiskey like water. They gave an occasional side glance at Slocum and Shorty, but then turned back to their own business. Slocum had not dismissed them, but he felt that until they gathered in enough whiskey to fortify their courage, he and Shorty were safe enough.

"Have some more whiskey," Slocum said, and poured it in his partner's cup.

"Be good to have them horses delivered and be on our way back home," Shorty said.

"Couple of days—"

"You over there, mister," one of the younger hunters said, and pointed at Slocum. He came across the room at an unsteady gait, and wobbled a little, obviously feeling his liquor.

He stopped and teetered on his heels. "Don't I know you?"

"Can't say that we have met," Slocum said, looking at the man mildly.

"Yeah, I do. You—you scouted for General Crook in Arizona."

Slocum agreed with a nod and settled a little, satisfied that the man had no large revelations to make from Slocum's past and didn't want to pick a fight.

"I was packing then," the hunter said.

"Camp Verde campaign?" Slocum asked, to make conversation.

"Yeah. Good to see you." The young man looked around as if he felt out of place standing there, and then went back to the bar.

"Yeah," Slocum heard the boy say out loud to his companions. "That's one tough sumbitch over there. I knowed him in Arizona."

Slocum almost smiled at the words. He hoped his reputation impressed Bergereon as much as it had that boy. They didn't need any problems over the corral. Hell, maybe he was only making a mountain out of a molehill.

Outside by themselves, he and Shorty walked back to their things. The night was dark and the muffled sounds of the noisy hunters carried outside.

"You figure they'll give us any trouble tonight?" Shorty asked under his breath with a quick check over his shoulder to be certain they were alone.

"I don't know, but I'm sleeping with one eye open," Slocum said.

"Good, I'll sleep with two closed and you wake me up before they start something."

"Go ahead and get some sleep." Slocum took a dark blanket and his Winchester. "I'm going to sit up a while."

"You itchy about them gents?"

"Just being careful."

Shorty agreed, and took his bedroll around on the opposite side of the corral.

Slocum nestled his back in the dark shadows against the corral, and under the blanket he sat back and waited. The penned horses snorted and stomped their hooves in sleep. Out on the prairie, Bergereon's mules fought, kicked, and squealed in the night. Further away, the buffalo wolves howled to each other in mournful refrains.

Some of the hunters staggered out of the store headed for their camp, and the shuffle of their feet jerked Slocum to awareness. Singing and laughing, they hardly sounded like a threat to keep him sitting up and awake.

"—two hundred new rifles. Lever action—"

He only heard part of their conversation. But two men were coming around the cabin and talking out loud about rifles.

"They're worth whatever we charge him for them."

"Can we get forty hides apiece for them?"

"Don't you worry. Sitting Bull will buy them and pay plenty!"

Then they were gone in the night. Had he overheard Bergereon and his man Randolph? Someone was going to sell the warring Sioux new rifles. If they were planning to sell Sitting Bull those guns, they damn sure were encouraging the Sioux to make war.

He sat under his blanket with his back against the rough post. Engrossed in his thoughts, he rubbed the itchy beard stubble around his mouth with the tip of his index finger.

Bergereon's business was not all hunting. Selling or trading rifles to hostile Indians was a serious offense—one that the military damn sure frowned on. But it was nothing to Slocum unless sometime he had to personally face those rifles.

A wolf howled closer to the outpost. Slocum nodded; he had heard him too. The buffalo hunters might not be going to bother their horses, but they aimed to upset things to satisfy their own greed.

3

The McBroom ranch didn't look out of the ordinary. They had a lodgepole over the gate and the MC brand burned in a board hung on it. A silvery-bladed windmill spun in the wind. Slocum led the way, riding the bell mare, heading toward the low log buildings, the cow ponies trailing behind. It didn't appear to be that impressive a place, and why McBroom needed four dozen cow ponies was beyond Slocum. But his wasn't to reason why anyway. Brady's horses were close to being delivered.

He watched a hatless blond woman hurry from the house to the corrals, no doubt to open the gates for them. She was tall, slender, her hair sun-bleached, and the silver shone bright on the concho belt that hugged her slim waist. Slocum stepped off the gray and removed his hat for her as the horses trotted past them through the gate.

"Howdy, Mrs. McBroom," he said over the whirl and clanks of the noisy mill.

"Oh, I'm not Mrs.," she said with a warm smile. "I'm Miss. I mean, Celia."

"Didn't know that," he said. "I'm sorry." Her being single increased his interest in her.

"No problem," she said, and extended her hand for him to shake. He felt his gut sink as he appraised her good looks and felt a stirring deeper than that. She was beautiful and

18

damned alluring, and her hand felt like the hand of someone who worked, but it also felt refined.

"This here is Shorty Giles, ma'am," Slocum said as the man reined up before them with a loud "Whew" and the last horse went inside the trap.

"This is Miss McBroom, Shorty."

"Ma'am, if he ain't said it, it is sure good to be here," Shorty said, inhaling loudly and dismounting heavily.

"Have any trouble?" she asked, her pale sky-blue eyes searching their faces.

"Some, not serious," Slocum said, dismissing the matter.

"My brother will be here in a little while. I'm surprised he hasn't come in already. He'll be grateful for these horses," she said, standing on the corral rails, leaning over the top rail and looking the animals over.

"Guess he's going to drive cattle?" Slocum asked, loosening his latigos.

"Yes, we have to deliver five hundred head of beeves to Ft. Robinson in the next sixty days."

"Getting late to do that, isn't it?" Shorty asked.

"Yes, but now we have the horses, we should make it with them before it gets real bad."

"Guess, he'll be back before long?" Slocum asked, looking around for sight of the man.

"Don't worry, Bruce'll be coming in any minute. Put your horses over in that pen and let them eat hay. I'll make some coffee and by then Bruce will be here, I'm certain."

"We can't refuse an invite from a pretty lady," Slocum said, and Shorty agreed with an enthusiastic nod.

"Celia," she reminded Slocum softly, and then smiled. "You unsaddle and unload your packs. By then the coffee will be piping hot."

"Celia—don't rush," Slocum said, and they exchanged a private look before she turned and hurried with her long corduroy skirt in her hand. He watched her small boot heels strike the ground as she hurried. The woman was sure a busy one.

"She's damn sure a looker," Shorty said. Then he ran his tongue around under his cheek. He spat something out and shook his head ruefully and whispered, "I'd give two, no, three months pay for one like her."

"You reckon there's anything that pretty back at that hog ranch we passed earlier today?" Slocum asked, teasing him.

"Did you see them homely gals that come outside?" Shorty stood on his toes to be sure she was out of earshot. "They was ugly as homemade sin. Whew, that was dirtiest lot of women I've ever seen. Some of them hog ranches are bad, but that was the worst one I ever came across. Them soldiers never have any money except on payday. I sure wasn't horny enough to ever stop there." Shorty finished unloading the first packhorse and piled the packsaddle on top of it.

Slocum had the other one unloaded and he unsaddled the gray mare, then put them in the pen. There was plenty of ripe prairie hay in the bunkers, and water in the trough that the windmill brought up and that flowed from the pipe. Shorty tossed his gear on the fence and Slocum closed the gate.

They washed up on the front porch. The rich lye soap felt good in Slocum's hands as he lathered and then rinsed them. He looked in the smoky mirror on the wall and regretted his whiskers. Well, you couldn't have everything. He took off his hat, arranged his hair, and shared a nod with Shorty.

Hat in hand, he went in the door.

"Put it on the wall there," she said, pointing.

He nodded and obeyed her. The sweet smells of donuts frying reached his nose. The rich scent settled in good and drew saliva in his mouth. His fortunes couldn't be better. The fresh aroma of coffee wafted in the room. All that and Celia's company to spice things up, as his aches and pains from the long trip vanished.

"Have a seat," she said, and indicated the table and straight-back chairs. "Could I coax you two into eating a few donuts?"

"Not without breaking our arms," Shorty said, rubbing his palms together.

They all laughed.

She poured them coffee in tin cups, and went back to her cooking on the stove. Slocum studied her long derriere. Why, he could almost span her waist with his hands. She glided across the floor with the platter of brown donuts for them.

"There, eat up, cowboys." Her lilting laughter sounded like a crystal bell. Her even teeth flashed like ivory with her smile. She could melt a blizzard, Slocum decided as he reached for his first donut. Why wasn't she married? She must be pushing thirty. That a woman so pretty could become an old maid was beyond him, unless Nebraska men were stone blind. There was something else there, he decided, gingerly lifting his first hot donut from the plate.

"Bruce is coming," she said as the sound of a horse approached.

"Good," Slocum said, and held up the half-eaten donut for her benefit. "This is sure wonderful."

"Yes, ma'am, it sure is," Shorty agreed, acting overwhelmed by the treat.

A large frame soon filled the doorway, and Slocum looked up and saw the man's brows knotted in disapproval. "You Texas trash bring in them horses?" he demanded. His cold glare was like an open challenge.

Slocum stared at the man for a moment. "We brought the horses you ordered." Then he rose to face the ill-tempered man head-on.

"Bruce, this is Slocum and Shorty Giles," she said in a tone of voice that sounded uncertain. Slocum didn't fail to note it. "I invited them in."

"Well, I'll pay them off and they won't have to stay any longer," McBroom snarled.

"Shorty, go load our horses," Slocum said under his breath, and he saw the lost look in the man's eyes, but Shorty obeyed him and hurried for the door with a clinking of his spurs. Slocum couldn't see her flush face. She stood at the stove cooking more donuts with her back to him. No doubt, she was embarrassed by her brother's curt way toward them. Obviously too, she was subservient to him.

McBroom came across the room from his desk and began to count out the money on the table. "Twenty-five hundred's what I owe you?" he asked, still sounding angry at their presence.

"That's what I understood was the sale price," Slocum said.

"I suppose they're all sound?"

"You can go look them over, count them, whatever you like."

"What good would it do?"

"Right. They're yours," Slocum agreed, and watched the man make piles of the bills. He didn't like to take all that cash, but he'd get it wired to Brady in Texas.

"Thank you for bringing them," Celia said, and picked up their cups.

"Huh? What are you thanking them for, Celia? They got paid for bringing them," her brother said brusquely.

"I was only being pleasant," she said, and went to the dry sink.

"Here it is, recount it if you like," McBroom said. "Then when you're through counting it, you two can ride on."

Slocum nodded that he'd heard the man. With great flair, he began to count the bills, taking his time to aggravate the man as much as possible. There was a strange situation here between him and his sister, more than just a protective one. Her brother actually acted jealous of them being there in the same room with her. Slocum licked his thumb and counted the next stack. Bruce McBroom was a bear-sized man, burly and with a reddish face the sun had tanned to one big freckle. Slocum guessed him close to her age. *One thousand.* Maybe her brother was the reason why Celia wasn't Mrs. Someone. He damn sure was possessive enough to be her husband, acting like she was only in her teens. *Fifteen hundred.* Slocum started on the next pile of bills, noting how the man had looked when he'd found them there with her. Across the table, McBroom shifted his weight from his right to his left boot, and made a wry, impatient scowl with his mouth.

Too bad if Slocum's counting aggravated him. He continued with deliberate care. His tally completed at last, he undid a button in his shirt and then stuffed the currency inside. McBroom by this time had posted himself between Slocum and Celia, so all he could see was his broad frame.

"Thank you, ma'am," Slocum said rather pointedly to the barrier that the man created with his bulk.

"You're welcome," she said softly. Slocum nodded, then turned on his heel. He took his hat from the rack, feeling himself being crowded out of the house. McBroom blocked the door behind him as he crossed to the horses and Shorty, already mounted.

Slocum checked the girth, satisfied, and out of habit, adjusted the .44 on his hip. He grasped the horn and vaulted into the saddle, and then looked a last time at the doorway. McBroom still blocked it; he wasn't letting her out, or letting them see her either.

"We damn sure wore out our welcome in a hurry here," Shorty said under his breath.

"Sure didn't take long. Let's ride," Slocum said, and set the gray mare into a lope. They would take her back to Texas; a good bell mare was worth plenty.

"He's damn sure saving Celia for hisself, ain't he?" Shorty asked as he peered back toward the house when they stopped at the gate.

Slocum dismounted and opened it for them. "Sure looks that way to me."

"Man, she can sure cook donuts." Shorty said, filing through with the two packhorses on the lead. "And she's pretty as any I've ever seen in a while."

Slocum agreed as he stared back at the distant house. He could still hear the clack of the windmill. Strangest deal he'd been into in a while. He shut the gate. Then they headed at a long trot for Ft. Cottonwood. Celia McBroom would be hard to forget. Something wasn't right back there at the MC Ranch, and it sure ate up his guts. Maybe Slocum was taken with her good looks, but he didn't know why a brother would act that way.

Maybe her brother simply hated Texans. There were lots of those people around, men who'd fought in the war against the South. No, McBroom just didn't want any other males around her. Slocum turned his face to the wind and felt the powerful mare under him. Winter was coming fast to this country. They'd better head back for San Antonio.

•   •   •

An hour later they rode past the hog ranch, a long, low adobe building with a sod roof, and several of the girls rushed out on the porch. One dove of ample girth wrapped in a blanket against the cold came out in the road. She put her hand familiarly on Shorty's leg and hurried along with him.

"Cowboy, you don't know what you are missing not stopping for me," she insisted, walking along beside his stirrup.

"I can't stop this time," he said, and looked dead ahead.

"How about you, big man?" she asked over the horse.

"Not today," Slocum said. "Not today."

"Well, if either of you two ever get horny, you come see Mary Lou!" she shouted after them.

"I'd damn sure have to be really horny to ever call on that sister," Shorty said under his breath when they were out of earshot.

Slocum's thoughts were on the pair they had left at the ranch. There was something unnatural there. Brothers and sisters normally didn't act like that. It was a shame too. She was a very alluring woman to look at.

4

"Slocum! Slocum!" someone shouted, and he was forced to turn in the saddle to see the man dressed in a blue officer uniform headed for him. Slocum made certain, looking around the streets of Ogallala, that no one else had paid undue attention to the man's shout. One could never be too careful; there might be a bounty hunter or someone in the crowd who recognized his name from a faded poster.

"Slocum, remember me?" the clean-shaven lieutenant said. "We met at Ft. Bowie. You and Tom Horn were scouting together then."

Slocum dismounted and shook the man's hand. "Sorry, but I can't recall your name."

"Schaeffer, Judson Schaeffer," the fair-haired man said, pumping Slocum's hand with enthusiasm. "What are you doing up here?"

"Brought a herd of cow ponies up from Texas for a rancher."

"You aren't interested in scouting some for the army, are you?" The straight-backed young cavalry officer was poised for his answer.

"I don't think so. I figure it'll soon get cold enough up here to freeze my thin blood."

"The army could sure use your talents," the man insisted.

"No, thanks."

"Who did you bring the horses up for?" Schaeffer asked.

"The McBroom ranch."

"Oh." The officer nodded his head solemnly.

"You know them?"

"I know this much. McBroom guards his sister like she was a wagon-load of gold." The man shook his head as if he knew more and wasn't telling.

"We learned that this morning, Shorty and me. What's the deal?"

"A lot of gossip is all I know." Schaeffer tried to dismiss it. "Say, we could sure use you in the army, wish you'd reconsider joining the scouts. We have a bunch of worthless ones on the payroll, and could use someone with your abilities."

"No, thanks. I need to transfer some money that I'm packing to a man in Texas, and then go try to chase down some of the trail dust that Shorty and I have accumulated the past two months."

"If you're still in the Paradise Saloon later on, I'll join you there."

"Good. I'll buy you a drink and we can talk about old times at Ft. Bowie," Slocum promised. "Remember, the Paradise," Slocum said to Shorty, and then he remounted as the lieutenant hurried off on his business.

"You fought them Apaches?" Shorty asked, sounding impressed as they stopped and dismounted before the Wells Fargo office.

"I chased them," Slocum said with a sigh. "They never stayed for many fights. They attacked, whipped our butts, and left. We spent most of our time looking all over hell for them."

At the Wells Fargo office, Slocum paid Shorty his hundred dollars in wages for the trip. He held out a hundred and fifty for himself, and sent the rest back to Brady in San Antonio, Texas, via Wells Fargo. Not bad wages for two months work. His obligation to Brady completed, they left their animals at the wagon yard and walked two blocks to the Paradise.

Slocum parted the swinging doors, went to the bar, and ordered a bottle of good rye from the barkeep. Then he selected a few cigars from the glass jar and paid the man. With two glasses and the bottle in his hand, he joined Shorty at a side table.

"Well, if you ain't the cutest pair of cowboys come in here in a while," the girl said, twirling the end of her shawl as she pranced around them. A brunette, she wore a low-cut red silk dress. She was short and thin, but interesting to look at. There was still enough of her youth left to entice a man.

"Have a seat," Shorty said with a wide grin, and swung a chair out for her to sit on.

"I reckon I will, since you boys look so nice," she said, and sat down between them. She hiked her dress up and then crossed her legs in a flash of bare flesh.

"What's your business in town?" she asked.

"Pleasure now," Shorty said with a slow grin.

"Well, you get ready for some. Billie, that's me." She smiled smugly at him. "I've got it all right up those stairs, friend." She fanned her fingers toward the ceiling. "Oh, boy, I can do things that you ain't never seen nor heard of."

Slocum drew out one of his cigars and offered another one to Shorty, who had scooted closer to her and was obviously more interested in her. He waved the offer of a smoke away. Slocum lit a lucifer and drew deep on his cigar. The rich smoke settled him as Shorty and the brunette began kissing.

Slocum knew it would not be long until Billie dragged his companion off to her web and extracted his venom. He savored his whiskey, tried to ignore the two, and thought with dread about the long boring ride back to south Texas. Only the thoughts of warm sunny days made the whole notion even worth his consideration.

"We'll be back," Shorty said, looking flushed as he followed the smug-faced dove away.

Slocum toasted him with his glass and sipped some more.

"There you are," Schaeffer said, coming in the bar.

"Get a glass," Slocum said to him. "Shorty will be back in a little while and he'll need his."

The lieutenant got his own tumbler from the bartender, and came over and took a seat. "The army is looking for gunrunners,'' he said abruptly. "Someone is trading these hostiles repeating rifles and ammunition.''

"Oh?"

"More than just hunting rifles too.''

"You have any notion who it is?''

"No, that's why I still wanted to see if you would go do some scouting for us, Slocum. You can get to and find places and people that a military man could never locate. We need to stop this gunrunning traffic with the hostiles out there. Would you take a scout's position and do that?''

"No, sir. I'm going back to Texas. Too cold up here for me.'' Slocum poured the man four fingers of rye in his glass.

The man nodded thanks and picked up his drink. "No way to convince you to work for even a few months on this?''

"I can tell you his name,'' Slocum said softly. He'd heard enough to help the man—and he damn sure owed nothing to the superior-acting buffalo hunter Bergereon.

"Oh, Jesus, you can?'' Schaeffer leaned over close to hear him. Excitement danced in his eyes.

"He'll be hard to catch at it. But his name is Simon Bergereon, and he's a buffalo hunter.''

"Bergereon, huh?''

"There may be more doing the same thing, but I overheard him telling someone about his next sale to Sitting Bull.''

"Sitting Bull? Oh, my aching backside. He's one of the biggest troublemakers of all we've got out here.''

"Bergereon won't be easy to catch either. He's tricky.''

"If you would work for us three months, we could close the book on all of those gunrunners.''

"Well, you have a good lead on one.'' Slocum raised his glass. He was ready to go find a barber, get a shave and a bath. What did Billie say earlier, she could do things upstairs . . . ? He thought about that.

"Slocum, thanks. I need to get back to my post. I sure wish you'd reconsider the offer.''

"I have money in my pants now,'' he said, and smiled at the man as he rose, downed his whiskey, and then prepared to leave.

"I sure owe you one now for that information," the lieutenant said, and hurried out.

"Where's a barber and bathhouse?" Slocum asked the bartender.

"Two doors down." The man pointed to the right of the bat-wing doors.

"Thanks. Oh, yeah, you send Shorty down there if he ever comes down from upstairs." Slocum stretched his tight back muscles and then he glanced at the stairs. Maybe he should have warned Billie about Shorty. He was hard to buck off.

He picked up his bottle, recorked it, and headed for the front door.

The smell of rose oil filled the steamy air in the bathhouse. The small mustached barber had cut his hair, and was starting to give him a shave when Shorty showed up.

"Whew, there you are," he said, coming in the shop.

Slocum handed him the bottle of rye from under the barber's shroud, and the bowlegged cowboy removed the cork and took a large dose from the neck. He ended that with a loud "ah" and handed the bottle back.

"You learn anything up there you didn't know?" Slocum asked.

"No, but it was sure fine. I guess I'm next to get the treatment?" Shorty asked the barber.

"Looks that way to me," Slocum said, and the barber smothered him with a hot towel.

"I'll be right with you," the man said to Shorty, and removed the boiling-hot cloth from Slocum's face. With a hog-bristle brush, he applied hot lather. Then he deftly finished scrapping Slocum's upper lip clean. He stood back and looked Slocum over critically before he did the rest.

"You ready for a bath?" the barber asked, the shave completed. He let down the chair and swept the cloth from Slocum.

"Suits me. I'll be back there," Slocum said to Shorty, and with his bottle in hand, he went through the curtained door to the bathing portion of the place.

Four copper tubs were lined in a row. The room was heavy

with the heat and steam. A Chinese boy came packing two wooden pails of hot water, and poured them in the first tub.

"You likey here?" he asked.

"Fine," Slocum said, beginning to undress. The notion of a good hot soaking made him feel sleepy. It would be nice to be clean for a change after two months on the trail.

"Me do clothes while you soaky?" the boy asked.

"Sure," Slocum agreed, and began to empty his pockets and hand the small Oriental his shirt, pants, and underwear. With the clothing over his arm, the boy swept up his socks, bowed, and disappeared.

Slocum eased his tall frame into the tub of steaming water, and then when he was settled he took another swig of the rye. This was high living. He set the bottle down on the chair beside the tub with his Colt, and relighted his cigar. He could hardly wait to hear Shorty's version of his romp with the dove Billie. Things seldom got better than this.

The knock on the hotel door awoke him from a sound sleep. What time was it? It was still dark outside the window. Damn, he was sure hung over. He rubbed his face, still not awake, sitting with his legs thrown over the side of the bed, his bare feet on the cool wood floor—where was he? Then came the knocking again.

"Yes, I'm coming," he called.

"Slocum?" said the muffled voice.

"Yeah, I'm coming," he said, pulling on his britches and going to answer the door.

He turned the entry key and then the knob. He was not prepared for the rush she made to get inside, and he staggered back a foot as she pushed herself into the room.

"Oh, thank God you haven't left yet," the out-of-breath Celia McBroom said, and closed the door.

He realized that his pants were not buttoned. However, with the door now shut, the room was fairly dim, only starlight coming in from the window. Standing face-to-face with her, he felt too self-conscious to finish dressing, so he swept his shirt off the chair, put it on, and quickly buttoned it. The bottom of the shirt would cover his fly—he hoped.

"What do you need?" he asked, then realized his words were too abrupt. He didn't know her purpose, and she wanted something—he knew that much—or she won't have crashed into his room.

"My brother has broken his arm and leg this afternoon in a buckboard accident. I have no one to turn to. Would you and that other Texas cowboy, Shorty—would you and him help me drive those steers to Ft. Robinson?"

"I kind of figured your brother didn't like having us around," Slocum said. He combed the hair back from his forehead with the fingers of his right hand. The smell of hair oil assailed him.

She drew a deep breath and then wet her lips. "Bruce is very protective. But . . ."

"Who's asking us to do this, you or Bruce?"

"Oh, me. Bruce doesn't even know I am here."

"Then how is he going to take to us helping you drive those cattle?"

"He is in lots of pain. The doctor—" She blinked her blue eyes. "He says laudanum will help, but Bruce won't be able to do anything but ride in a wagon."

Slocum shook his head. She didn't get his point. "You still didn't tell me how he was going to like us helping you herd the cattle."

"He has no choice. We have to get those cattle to Ft. Robinson. We have a mortgage on the ranch. We will lose everything if we don't deliver those cattle. We have no other way to repay it but deliver the cattle to the army and agency."

"He was sure an angry man the day he found us with you," Slocum said. He wanted answers and lots of them. Pretty woman or not, he needed answers if she expected him to help her.

"I can handle him. I need some experienced drovers. I have two young boys to help us. That's all they are is farm boys, but they can ride. Bruce planned for them to go along and help us." She looked so helplessly at Slocum that it gnawed at his guts.

"I've never been there before," he said to warn her.

"Where?" she asked.

"Ft. Robinson."

"I have a map, and we drove cattle up there two years ago."

"Good, leave the map with me."

"You mean you will drive them up there?" A look of hope glinted in her blue eyes.

"I don't work for Bruce, understand?" He waited for her reply. This would be the test. No way would he undertake a drive like that and put up with her jealous bully of a brother.

"I understand."

"Who's in charge? Someone must be in charge. One person."

"You can be the trail boss," she said softly.

"Good, that's settled. Do you have plenty of provisions for the trip?"

"I am getting them. Yes, I will have, and I have a good cook hired too."

"Are the horses all shod?"

"No—do they have to be?" She frowned, and a concerned line formed on her smooth forehead.

"Yes, they do. You better get a keg of horseshoes and nails. We'll need to do that first. You can't expect a horse to hold up working cattle barefoot, even in Nebraska."

"How long will that take?"

"A couple of days. If Shorty's back and mine hold out. Get those boys over to your place in the morning. They can help us shoe them."

"Ah—but I haven't told Bruce yet." She dropped her gaze to the floor.

"Celia." He looked at her hard. This matter of Bruce being told and agreeing had to be settled, or Slocum wasn't going to take the job.

"I know," she said, "but he'll be fighting mad over this."

"Then you better dose him up with the medicine. And Celia?"

"Yes?"

"Take him several bottles. I don't want to worry about cattle and him on my back too."

"Oh, he'll understand in time."

"I ain't counting on it."

"I'll handle it. I promise you will be in charge. Thanks," she said with a pleased smile to dismiss his concern. Impulsively she stood on her toes, cupped his face in her hands, and kissed him tenderly on the mouth. Then, in a whirl of her hip-hugging blue serge skirt, she was out the door.

He stood there knifing in his shirt with his hands, and finally buttoned his pants as he considered her. Celia McBroom and her mad brother. How far was it from Ogallala to Ft. Robinson anyway? He tasted her on his lips and smiled. He'd better go break the news to Shorty. They weren't going straight home to Texas.

5

His head hurt, and he hated rye whiskey. Shorty didn't look any better swaying in the saddle than Slocum felt. Somewhere off in the east, a purple-yellow sky beckoned the start of dawn; they were headed for the MC Ranch. A thick silver frost coated the brown-grass sea that rolled away from them.

"So she came and hired you to drive her cattle to Ft. Robinson?" Shorty asked.

Slocum repeated what he had told him the night before after he'd found Shorty frolicking around in his underwear in the parlor of Lucy Dennison's house of ill repute with a brunette called Suey.

"You knew damn good and well," Shorty said, "that it's going to be winter one of these days up here, and I planned to spend that portion of the year in Texas. South Texas, to be exact, not up here getting an Injun arrow in my ass or freezing it off in damn blizzards."

Slocum twisted in the saddle and looked into the man's bloodshot eyes with a scowl of disgust. "Quit your bitching, Shorty, and ride up here with me. I'm damn tired of having to turn around to talk to you."

Shorty booted his horse up beside him.

"What happened to her brother?" Shorty asked with a pained expression as if the entire matter had him confused.

"Got a broken leg and arm," Slocum said. "Damn, I don't

34

know much more than you do. I ain't planning to spend all winter up here. Just simply get her cattle to Ft. Robinson, and then we can go where it's warm.''

"Good.'' Shorty turned up his jumper collar to the wind. "Damn sight colder today than it's been so far, and I figure it ain't half as cold as it'll get before we deliver those beeves to that fort.''

"It'll get a lot colder than this.'' Slocum rose in the stirrups. "Let's trot.''

They reached the MC Ranch gate and rode down the lane. Slocum kept a wary eye on the low-walled house as they approached it. Even though Bruce McBroom might be laid up with a broken arm and leg, he still might not agree with his sister's decision.

"What's first?'' Shorty asked, looking around as a collie came out and barked at them.

"Shoe those horses.''

"Them broncs we brought up here?'' The tone of his voice showed disbelief.

"Yes, that's their horses.''

Shorty shook his head, then stared off toward the east. "I thought I was done with them crow-baits.''

"Just getting started,'' Slocum said, and dropped from his horse.

Celia hurried from the house. "Morning, gents. The boys will be here in a little while.''

"Morning, ma'am,'' they both said.

"You had breakfast?'' she asked.

"No,'' Shorty said. "He got me up too danged early.''

"Come inside. I figured you'd not have eaten.''

"How's your brother?'' Shorty asked.

"Oh, he's still at Doc Morgan's in town.''

Shorty and Slocum exchanged a confident nod of approval as they followed her inside. Warmth from the fireplace struck Slocum's shaven face as he hung up his hat and began unbuttoning his canvas coat. The fresh smell of coffee and the aroma of pancakes cooking on a griddle made him feel that the ride out there had been worth it.

"I bought the shoes and the nails. Bruce has a forge and anvil if you need to shape them," she said, pouring coffee for them between checking on her pancakes.

He enjoyed watching her long slender hips sway while she worked about the iron range. Shorty had gone to warm his hands at the fireplace, and stood as if absorbing every degree of heat the radiant fire put out.

"Crisp morning," she said, handing Slocum a plate of steaming cakes. "Butter and syrup is on the table."

"Thanks," he said with a smile, and looked into her clear blue eyes.

"Better eat them while they're hot," she said, but never looked away.

"I'll do that," he said, and stepped to the table.

"I'll have yours ready in a minute," she said to Shorty, who had turned around and was warming his backside with the heat.

"No rush, ma'am. Them horses will still be out there."

"I just told Shorty we needed to nail on some shoes to-day," Slocum said.

"Oh," she said, and busied herself with the griddle and cooking.

"It wasn't bad enough we had to drive them up here," Shorty said. "Now we have to shoe them." He shook his head and looked at his scuffed boot toes.

The aroma of her syrup made Slocum forget about his partner's griping. He sliced out a pie-shaped piece of pancake with his fork, and before the morsel passed his lips, the saliva drowned his mouth. This was the kind of food he hadn't had in a long time. Afterwards, he took a sip of the hot rich coffee and nodded to her. "It's sure good."

She smiled and turned the new pancakes over. "You don't like to shoe horses, Shorty?"

"I don't really like to work at all, but ma'am, for those pancakes, I'd almost build a fence."

Shorty's words drew warm laughter from her. It peeled like a small silver bell, and Slocum looked up to see sparkles in her blue eyes. She handed Shorty his platter and turned back to cook some more.

The dog barked outside; she turned and listened. "It must be the boys coming."

"Want me to let them in?" Slocum asked, rising from his chair.

"Sure," she said. "They probably haven't eaten either."

"Come on in," Slocum shouted to them from the doorway.

The boys looked to be in their mid-teens. They were dressed warmly and carried fat bedrolls tied on behind their saddles. They both wore scotch caps with earflaps and bills, along with leather sheepskin-lined coats. They dismounted and hurried to the door.

"Morning, sir," the younger one said as he hurried by him.

"That's Thad and I'm Barley Burns," the second and older one said to Slocum. He drew off a glove and shook Slocum's hand. "Where's Bruce?" he asked in a lowered voice.

"He had an accident and is at Dr. Morgan's," Slocum said.

"Oh, that's why we're allowed inside, huh? He ain't here then?"

Slocum shared a wink with the youth, and they both went into the main room.

"Did you meet Mr. Slocum?" she asked.

"Yes, ma'am."

"Then wash up, and I'm making more pancakes. Bruce won't be able to make this drive and I've hired Mr. Slocum to lead it."

"Just call me Slocum, boys," he said to set them at ease.

"It won't hurt us to be polite," Thad said. "Our father would want it that way."

"Fine, but if you call Shorty anything but Shorty, he might get grumpy."

"What!" Shorty looked up from his eating and looked around as if he'd missed the whole thing.

"This is Thad and Barley Burns, Shorty. They're going to ride with us to Ft. Robinson."

"Good. Nice to meetcha." He went back to eating.

Slocum cradled his coffee cup as the two boys took their places at the table. "We need to shoe all the horses first," he said. "We'll start doing that today."

"Them new horses very wild?" the younger one asked, looking wary.

"They're part she-wolf and the other part bobcat," Shorty said. "I'll bet half them horses is here on account of they didn't like to be shod. So they sold them to Jim Brady." Shorty shook his head, never looking up from his plate.

"If they are, we'll lay them down and shoe them that way," Slocum said, wishing Shorty wouldn't scare the boys away from what they had to do.

"Will you have to do many of them like that?" Thad asked.

"Half of them, boy. Half of them," Shorty said with a finality to his words that sounded fatal. "We'll be lucky if that's all. By the way, ma'am, how did your brother get hurt?"

"The new team of mules he bought and was breaking to pull the chuck wagon ran off with the buckboard and wrecked it and him both."

Slocum closed his eyes at the latest revelation. They had a team of mules to break too before they ever left for Ft. Robinson.

6

Celia worked the bellows and kept the coals red hot in the forge for Slocum. The table made of iron was sloped to the center, stood on four pipe legs, and had a shield to divert the wind. Slocum stacked several shoes around in the heated center at one time. The Burns boys rasped and trimmed the hooves for him to fit the plates on them. On horseback, Shorty roped and brought the animals out of the pen. They worked like a team, and Slocum could see the boys would pull their own weight.

Slocum checked the mid-morning sun. They had shod a dozen, and had three dozen left. The horses that Shorty had chosen to draw out of the corral so far had been using horses with white scars from saddle sores on their withers. Obviously he was saving the wilder ones until last. Slocum never looked up. He was stripped down to only his shirt, the exertion of his labor proving enough to warm him despite the chilly wind. Not to mention the forge's blast in his face when he used the pincers to draw out a hot shoe and beat it to fit a particular hoof.

The bell-like clanging of his hammer on the surface rang in his ears as he straightened the iron plate to lie flat under each horse's hoof. Then, when he was satisfied with the fit, he nailed it in place.

''I've shod several of our horses at home for my dad,''

Barley offered. "Thad can keep up now on the trimming."

"Good. Get a hammer and some nails and try that dun—he's quiet enough."

"Where's the wild ones, sir?" Barley asked quietly.

"I think Shorty's saving them for last." Slocum cast a glance as the man delivered another cow pony to the other Burns boy to trim.

Barley agreed with a sharp nod and went to work.

"It's going fast," Celia said, and flexed the bellows until the coals in the center glowed red.

"We're getting there," Slocum offered, still unsure about how the last ones to be shoed in the herd would act.

"You don't brag much, do you?" she said softly.

"No, ma'am." Then he rapped the hammer on the side of a shoe that was too wide. Not satisfied with the malleability of the metal, he stuck the iron oval back in the coals to heat some more.

"You aren't just a cowboy, are you?" she asked as he wiped the beads of sweat from his forehead on his sleeve. The strong fumes of the burning coal made his eyes water. He stepped back and cleaned them with the corner of his kerchief.

"I've scouted, freighted, trapped, and hunted too."

"No," she said quietly, and acted interested in the forge's contents. "You aren't *just a cowboy*."

"Pretty much how I earn my keep."

"You're educated."

"Does it show?"

"No, but I can tell you have some education."

"Excuse me," Barley said, leading the shod dun up for his inspection. "He look all right?"

"Did a great job. Go get another and bring me one too." Slocum turned to her when the boy was out of hearing. "Have you ever been married?" he asked, pausing for her reply.

"No."

"So we both have secrets."

She squeezed on the leather bellows, and the purple-reddish flames rose at the center of the forge. "Come to the house tonight when the others are asleep,'' she said in a low voice for him alone to hear. "We can talk then.''

"I may be too tired.'' He shared a private look with her. She was serious. He doubted he would ever be that tired—but this farrier work was strenuous, and night was a long way off.

"Then I will understand,'' she said, and turned back to tending the forge.

He nodded that he'd heard her, and by then Barley was back. Slocum took the lead of the big snorty bay from the boy. This one would be a real challenge.

Slocum hitched the gelding to the ring on the post and moved down his side, speaking softly as he ran his hand over the horse's rump and started down his leg; he barely side-stepped the animal's cow-kick.

"That's the one you've been looking for,'' she said from behind him.

"Easy,'' he said, not answering her, his attention centered on the bay and what the animal would try next. At last, with the bay's hind foot cradled in his lap, he eyeballed the smoothed-off hoof for a fit. He'd be lucky if this one didn't kick his head off. The bay began to lean on him as he tried the shoe on his hoof and took a look at how the plate had to be shaped to fit it. Slocum let the hoof drop; he'd seen enough. When he picked it up again, it would be the next-to-last time he lifted that hoof.

"He's a tough one, sir,'' Thad shouted from his position bent over and rasping on another hoof.

"I see that already.'' Slocum straightened. He had seen enough shoes that he could almost fit one by looking at the shape of the hoof. He took a cold shoe and raised the bay's other hind leg despite some protesting kicks. If they didn't get worse than this, he could handle them.

"I'm going to fix lunch,'' Celia announced. "Can you handle the forge and shoes too?''

"We'll make it,'' he said. He watched her hurry toward the house. Lots of woman in that long divided skirt. Then he turned his attention back to shoeing until she rang the triangle.

"We going to finish tomorrow?" Shorty asked as they washed up at the table outside the front door.

"We may have some left to do after today."

"The way I ache, I figure this weather is going to change."

"Yes, and we need to be moving out. We still have those mules to break," Slocum said with a wry shake of his head.

"The ones he had the wreck with?" Shorty scowled at him.

"Only mules I know about that she owns. They down in the pens?"

"Yeah, I looked them over and they're snorty," Barley said under his breath, and then they went inside.

Her beef and potato stew hit the spot. Through the meal, Slocum considered how much longer it would take to finish the shoeing. His back had a catch in it, and he knew for his part he'd be glad to have it over with.

"Guess we all could shoe this evening," Shorty offered, and drew a nod from the others.

"We thought you'd forgot how," Slocum said over his fresh cup of coffee, and drew laughter from everyone.

"Those mules, have they ever been broke?" Slocum asked Celia as she hustled around refilling their cups.

"We used them last year to pull the chuck wagon up there. But Bruce tried to mow with them this summer, and they tore up the mowing machine with him on it, so he turned them out until day before yesterday." She stood ready with the granite pot in her hand waiting for an empty cup.

"After we get through shoeing, I guess breaking those mules to drive is next."

"I don't know, she said, sounding concerned. "Perhaps I should buy a new team."

Slocum shook his head. "They're mules. They can be broke."

"I don't need anyone else hurt."

"We'll handle the mules." He looked over, and the Burns boys gave him an affirmative nod. No mules were going to whip them either.

With the shoeing down to the last few head in the late afternoon, he headed for a serious look at the mules. Slocum knew lots about mules. The animals were typically hard-headed, and the two large black mules chewing on hay in the back pen were large animals too, perhaps sixteen hands. Powerful enough to do as much damage as good pulling the loaded chuck wagon. He had seen the torn-up harness and buckboard they'd run off and wrecked. It was a sobering reminder that they were big and wild.

"That's Jubal and Teddy," Celia said, joining him on the corral fence. "Jubal has the star."

"I'm going to hitch them to the chuck wagon in the morning," he said, considering the rest of his plans for the pair.

"What if they wreck that?"

"They won't. I'm using a lodgepole to lock the back wheels, and they can wear themselves out dragging it all over hell like a big sled."

"Will it work?" she asked, looking at him mildly for his reply.

"We'll know tomorrow, won't we?"

"I guess we will," she said, and her pale blue eyes held his gaze for a long time.

7

Somewhere out on the prairie, a wolf howled. The sky was lighted with a thousand stars as Slocum hurried in the cold night air for the house. He was amazed how his strength had returned after Celia's filling supper. Many of his aches and pains had fled at the prospect of meeting with her alone. He'd left Shorty snoring in the top bunk, and the boys asleep in their beds, when he quietly put on his hat and coat and eased out the bunkhouse door.

A rap on her front door, and he waited in the gray night. The ghostly outline of the corrals and grunts of sleeping horses stomping in their new shoes filled the night. She might have gone to—

"Come in," she said, and peered out to be certain he was alone. The high-neck blue dress molded her trim body and swirled around her slender form as she moved.

"Just me," he said, removing his hat and putting it on the peg by the door.

"I'm glad you came after all. I was afraid you'd be too tired. Take off your coat," she said, and smiled at him. "Would you have some whiskey?"

"A glass would be fine," he said as he shrugged off his coat and hung it beside his hat. The warmth of the blazing fireplace filled the snug great room and drove the night's chill from his face.

"I guess you think I'm brazen inviting you up here by yourself?" She glanced over her shoulder at him as she drew down the brown bottle from the cupboard shelf.

"I guess two adults can speak to each other," he said, taking a chair at the wooden table where she indicated.

"I would think so." She poured him some whiskey in a tin cup and then she delivered it. "Supposed to be good whiskey. I never drink any, so I couldn't tell you."

"It isn't rotgut," he said after a sip.

She sat across from him and chewed on her lower lip. Then she recrossed her legs under the table and acted uncomfortable.

"Something bothering you, Celia?" he asked, looking into her pale blue eyes.

"Yes. You are. Bruce always says I am a poor judge of men—" She bolted up and went to the fireplace and put more wood on the fire.

He moved to stand over her. She glanced at the blazing fire, and at last up at him. Then she rose and he held out his arms, and she moved inside them. Her hands cupped his face and she kissed him. He tasted the honey in her mouth and crushed her to his chest.

"I'm glad you didn't ask more—" she said, out of breath, her face buried in his shirt.

"You can tell me whatever you want me to know," he said, holding her by the waist and savoring her closeness.

"Not now," she said, shaking her head firmly, and led him by the hand to the lame bed against the wall.

She looked at him for a long moment, then after hesitating, began to unbutton her dress. Then she paused and looked up furtively at him. "Am I too forward for you?"

"No." He undid his gunbelt and hung it on the chair.

"Would you turn your back for a minute longer?" she asked. "I promise not to run away, but while I may act as if I have no shame, I am embarrassed for you to see me undressed."

"I'll do that." He kept his back to her as he undid his shirt and then shoved down his galluses. He toed off his boots, and heard the bed ropes protest behind him when she climbed on it.

"You can turn around now," she said, seated on the bed and holding the blankets up to her throat.

"I'll blow out the lamp," he said.

"Yes, thank you," she said quietly.

The lamp extinguished, he came back and stripped off his pants and underwear. Red-orange firelight danced on the ceiling and the roof cross braces; he climbed in the bed and slid under the cool clean covers.

She squirmed toward him, and the cool touch of her long slender breasts burned holes in his chest. He drew in a ragged breath and then sought her mouth. His hand molded her flesh, and she sighed as their lips pressed hard together. Their hunger raged like a fire until between gasps of her short breath, she pleaded for him to take her.

He raised up, moved over on top of her, and then knelt between her spread-apart knees. His throbbing manhood swung like a pendulum until he captured it and nosed it home into her wet slot. She cried out loud at his entry, and her fingernails dug into the skin on his back. Her sharp moans of "yes, yes" only encouraged him to go faster. They sought to extract the deepest pleasure from each other in their wild abandon. The bed ropes screamed in protest as he sought the bottom of her well.

His breath raged in hoarse gasps and his plunging hips ached from the day's horseshoeing, but they both were one and going downhill at bobsled speed. Her legs wrapped around him as she hunched her muscular stomach and slender butt toward him for more and more.

"Oh, Slocum!" she cried out, stiffening under him, and then she fainted in a limp heap.

He held himself up, huffed in hard breaths, and grinned down at her as she shook her dazed head. The cool air of the room swept his bare skin, and he absently drew the cover up over himself with one hand to hold in some of their body heat.

"I never do that," she said in dismay. "I never faint."

"Kind of nice?" he said with a grin, then pushed himself back into her depths.

"Yes." She pulled him down on top of her and kissed him wetly. "You may not get any sleep at all tonight," she said. Then a wicked smile crossed her face and she kissed him again.

They lay on their sides face-to-face, resting. He studied the glow of the fireplace on the underside of the ceiling, and carefully pushed the wisps of sun-bleached hair back from the side of her face.

"Do you and him share this bed?" he asked softly.

"Yes. That's a sin too, isn't it?"

"I ain't a preacher. I don't quote the Bible. Just curious."

"We have been lovers for years," she said. "But you already knew that, didn't you?"

"I knew there was only one bed in this room."

"Dead giveaway, isn't it? Bruce and I discovered each other years ago after our parents died. He kept saying we had to find mates someday, but now I fear he doesn't want to find anyone."

"So he controls you?"

She rolled over on top of him. "Yes, he does. Let's not talk about that now, please." Her pained show of disappointment threatened to shatter their contentment. Then a look of mischievous discovery spread over her face in the firelight, and she squirmed on top of him.

Her hand reached down and sought his half-erect shaft. She pulled on it. "I think he is waking up again."

"Yes, maybe he is." He laughed out loud at her furious tugging on his tool.

"You know, Slocum, I've never ever enjoyed it this much before."

"Good," he said as she straddled his stomach and inserted his sword inside her. With it in place, she began to bounce on him.

"That feels good," she said, and reached down underneath and squeezed the base of his root hard. "He's filling up."

"Yes," he said, feeling the deep soreness from the shoeing in his back and legs nag at him as they began all over again.

This time he found relief and came inside her in an explosion. She dropped off him when they finished. He curled around her naked form and cuddled her right breast in his hand.

"Will we wake up before they do?" she asked dreamily.

"You worried about your reputation?"

"No!" She caught him by the backside and pulled him closer to her butt. "I want to do it again before they come to breakfast."

He looked at the ceiling for help. Oh, well, someday they would get those steers to Ft. Robinson.

After breakfast found Slocum and the others harnessing the mules. With a twitch on each mule's upper lip, and one of the Burns boys holding each of the walleyed jackasses, the animals stood only feet apart, making whistling noises out of their noses. Slocum and Shorty bridled and harnessed them while the boys contained them. Under the twitches, they stood quietly enough to be manageable. Then, still in the nose holds, the team was led to the tongue and hitched to the wagon. A lodgepole securely tied across the rear wheels served as a brake. The mules had to skid the rear wheels to move it.

Shorty ran to get on his horse to head them off should they run away, and Slocum climbed on the seat with the lines. The Burns boys released the mules and quickly stepped back.

"Be careful," Celia shouted at him from the porch, drying her hands on a towel.

The mules plunged into the collars and jerked the wagon up with the leather tugs, and when the wheel-lock took hold, they were tossed back on their butts. They charged to their feet and began to dig in, but obviously it would be no runaway this time, and they seesawed a few times until Slocum brought them together with the reins.

The two mules dropped down to pull, and began to skid the wagon. Slocum nodded to Shorty, who was ready to rope the runaways if they broke loose.

"I believe they'll soon get tired of dragging this wagon all over Nebraska," Slocum said.

Shorty agreed. Slocum watched Celia head for the house after giving her approval. Nice-looking rump on that gal, and she sure was different than any other he had ever tangled with. If Bruce ever got well enough to come home, Slocum might have to fight him. He'd have to see what time would bring.

Members of the crew took turns driving the mules. Soon the team acted as if they had enough work not to run off at the first jump, so the brake on the wheels was removed. Barley drove the team, and Thad was the outrider to capture them if they ran away. Slocum felt satisfied that with training the mules would work out.

After the noon meal, Celia and Slocum saddled horses to ride out to check on the steers. They were scattered across the brown-grass prairie, but he felt convinced as they rode through them that the steers could be gathered in a day and shaped into a herd. A few of the wilder ones rose at their approach, and ran to the nearest high ground before they turned to look back.

"Spooks," Slocum wryly commented more to himself than her. If possible, he planned to cull that kind out of the herd. He rose in the stirrups and began to trot his horse. A cold wind swept his face and reminded him winter wasn't far away and they had to trail north. There were still more steers to look at.

They returned to the house in the last rays of sundown. Shorty and the boys had improvised for their own supper.

"We butchered a fat barren heifer for beef," Shorty said as Slocum and Celia inspected the carcass hanging on the poles in the yard. It was spotted with slabs of fat, and Slocum knew that the man had made a good choice. The meat would be tender.

"Good idea," she agreed. "I'll have us some supper ready in a minute," she said to Slocum, giving him the reins to her horse and ducking inside the house.

"I'll be there," Slocum asked.

"How do them steers look?" Shorty asked, rubbing his mouth with his fingers.

"Fat longhorns. They have really done well up here on this

grass. A few spooks, but I figure we can break most of them. They were driven up here sometime, and once they get back to being driven again, they should settle down. Besides, they are fat and that will slow them a lot more than thin Texas cattle fresh off the range.''

"Good. Them boys is workers and they'll do to ride with," Shorty said, looking to check that they couldn't hear his words.

"Figured that yesterday when we shod the horses. They don't back up from work," Slocum agreed. "You and the older one will ride swing. The other boy and I'll will keep them coming.''

He joined Celia in the house for supper. The others went to the bunkhouse. With care, he washed his hands and face, dried them on her towel, and then with a nod at her smile, took a seat at the table.

"You get the rest of the supplies tomorrow," he said. "We'll gather those cattle and the next day head north.''

"It may be hard to leave Bruce," she said, sounding unsure.

"Whatever. He sure won't be comfortable riding in that wagon.''

"I know but he's—he'll be jealous.''

"I don't intend to put up with much ranting and raving.''

She nodded her head in short bobs. "I don't want you to have to either. I promised you—''

"Do whatever you have to," he said, and lifted the warm coffee cup before him in both hands. No way would he go on the drive with her brother along—but he'd decide that when the time came. There wasn't room on this drive for him and Bruce.

8

The bawling of the cattle in their ears, Slocum and Shorty were sitting their horses and making a final tally of a large group of steers. The sunset fired the bottoms of the low-stacked clouds on the western horizon. Stretched out before them, 750 prime, fat longhorns filled the creek bottom. Both of the Burns boys were dismounted and venting their bladders.

"We actually have seven hundred sixty-eight head," Slocum announced. "That will handle some losses on the trail, and she's got thirty head of wild haints left here."

"Glad we don't need to take them real spooky ones," Shorty said, gripping his saddlehorn and rocking in the saddle to stretch out his stiffness.

"Worked out fine," Slocum agreed. "Boys, them steers won't go anywhere tonight. Come sunup, we'll be ready to head them up and trail them north."

"You ever been to Ft. Robinson?" Barley, the elder of the two, asked.

"No, but I figure it's up there." Slocum gave a toss of his head to the north.

"We been there once. They say Crazy Horse is up there too. You know him?" The boy's green eyes narrowed at the corners, and the serious look on his face showed his concern.

51

Not fear-ridden, but an honest matter-of-fact man-to-man question.

Slocum shook his head. "Nope, never met him. Why?"

"I figure he might want to go on the warpath before we get there, and then what?"

"The army might not need these steers in that case," Slocum said, wondering what the boy's point was in this conversation.

"I sure wasn't itching to die yet. You ever think about that?"

"I have many a time, but you know, when your number comes up I truly doubt that you can change it."

"You mean that if I'm supposed to die on this drive, nothing, not even prayers, can change it?"

"Sounds kind of final." Slocum reined the big horse around to face the youth. "But that's the way I see life and death. Let's get to the ranch. We may have to cook our own supper again if Celia ain't back from town with those supplies."

When they rode in, Slocum noticed the buckboard parked at the corral. A twinge of dread grabbed at his guts as he heavily dismounted and began to undo the girth. Had Bruce come home with her? The lights inside the main house glowed yellow through the narrow bottle windows. They were frontier answer for a shortage of panes. The builder simply notched out a space in the logs and lined glass jars in a row to let in light.

He saw the front door open, and Celia flung a shawl over her shoulder and rushed out to the corrals. He hesitated, dropping the girth, and waited for her.

"How did it go?" she asked them.

"Got the mules settled some more. And we have the steers in the creek bottom ready to move out come first light, Miss Celia."

"We're ready to start north?" she asked Slocum softly, hugging her arms in the gathering darkness.

"I think we can start in the morning. Did Bruce come home?"

"Yes," she said in a small voice. "How did you know?"

"I figured as much the way you were acting." Slocum looked for a long moment at the dark outline of the main house, then reached down and drew the girth back up. "I'll get my things and be gone."

"Oh, you can't—"

"I don't intend to ride to Ft. Robinson with him along."

"Oh, please give him a chance. He's an invalid. His right arm's in a cast and his right leg too. He can't even walk on crutches."

"Don't matter. There can only be one boss on a drive. I'll get my things and head out."

"But you haven't even eaten," she pleaded.

"Thanks, Celia. We made an agreement. Him or me. It won't work any other way."

"Guess I'll be going too, ma'am," Shorty said. "I ain't working for him either." He shook his head ruefully.

"Celia! Celia!" Bruce called to her from the house.

"You better go answer him," Slocum said as she looked undecided at the house, then back at them.

"Ma'am, guess if Slocum isn't the boss we'll have to quit too," Barley said.

"All of you! All of you are up and quitting on me?" She looked in disbelief at them.

"Yes, ma'am, but it ain't you—it's him!"

"But how will I—? Oh, please reconsider."

Slocum turned his back; she had made her decision. He led the bay toward the bunkhouse. Her lamenting pleas at last were silenced as her brother's calling grew louder, and Slocum heard her soft footfalls as she ran to the house. *Better go wait on him.* At the hitch rack before the bunkhouse, Slocum slung on his bedroll, tied it down, and then hung his war bag on the horn. He shook the boys' hands.

"I'm sorry, fellas, but I struck a deal with her to drive the cattle up there without him."

"We understand and we ain't working for him neither," Barley said.

"She can hire her some cowboys in town," the younger Burns boy offered. "I've seen a few left up here who ain't got the money to go home, I guess."

"She'll get a bunch of no-accounts," Shorty said under his breath.

"That ain't our worry," Slocum added.

"Right."

Slocum shared some hard jerky from his saddlebags with the others. They shook hands and mounted up. The boys prepared to head for home, and the two men were ready to ride to town.

"This damn jerky must have been sawed off of a tough steer," Shorty complained as he gnawed on his piece and tried to jerk it apart from his clenched teeth.

"Beats nothing," Slocum said, and threw a leg across the bay. He still had the gray mare and two packhorses to get out of the corral.

"Wait! Wait!" Celia cried, running pell-mell toward them in the deepening darkness. "Bruce isn't going. He's agreed to stay here."

Slocum reined up his horse. The animal snorted wearily.

"Wait!" she cried, out of breath, and braced herself with her hands on the side of his horse.

"He's not going?" Slocum asked.

"He can't go. He can't even walk."

"Who is going to run the drive?"

"You are, of course."

Slocum dismounted. "Fine. I don't aim to work for him. I told you that once. I won't repeat it." He paused for her promise again.

"He understands. Now all of you come to the house and eat supper."

"If Slocum's the boss, we'll stay," one of the boys volunteered.

"Yeah, same goes for me. I hate this jerky he serves anyway," Shorty said in disgust.

The meal was quiet. Bruce sat and sulked in the chair by the fireplace. Both his right arm and leg were in splints and bandages, and he had lost most of his usual menace as he slumped in the chair. Slocum ignored him.

"We'll head out in the morning," Slocum said to her.

"Yes, I loaded the supplies in the chuck wagon this afternoon. In the morning, we can put that beef in. The cook, Adolph, will be here at daybreak.''

"We would have helped you transfer the supplies,'' Shorty said.

"I usually load things by myself,'' she said as she delivered the platter of steaming oven-brown biscuits to the table.

The air in the house drew taut as a fiddle string, everyone talking carefully and expecting any minute that something would spark the silent Bruce, but the meal passed without incident.

After supper, she held Slocum back as she stood outside the door and waited until the others were gone on to the bunkhouse.

"We—I need to get those steers to Ft. Robinson.''

"I understand. How will he care for himself here alone?'' He motioned toward the doorway and the shaft of light that leaked on to the porch boards.

"He won't listen to me about bringing in a nurse to care for him.''

"That's his own hardheadedness then.'' Slocum shook his head; he'd lose no sleep over the man's welfare if that was how he wanted it.

"Oh,'' she said in a low voice, sounding sad. "I don't know what I'd do if anything happened to him.''

"Will someone come by and check on him?''

"Yes, Doc will.''

"Then don't worry. If he gets too bad off, maybe the doc can get him to listen, or take charge.''

"Yes, but going off—'' She turned her ear as he called to her again.

"Breakfast before dawn?'' Slocum reminded her.

"I'll have it ready. I better go. Thanks,'' she said, then took his arm and kissed him on the cheek.

"Don't thank me yet,'' he said over his shoulder, and went through the starlight to the bunkhouse breathing clouds of vapor in the frigid night air.

Sunup came with a cold wind. Frost coated the brown grass and crunched under their boot soles and horse hooves. A big hulk of a man with German accent, Adolph was there and helped her fix the breakfast. After a session with everyone helping hitch the mules, Adolph accepted the team warily. When the mules were ready and he was on the seat, Shorty and Thad mounted, ready to head off the snorting team if they tried anything.

Adolph clucked to the mules as if they were a team of well-broken Belgians, and they took to the collars, crowding the neck yoke, and the wagon began to roll. Slocum could see the man had handled tougher mules before and this was his business.

"Ten miles or so today?" Adolph asked above the rattle of the wagon.

"That'll be far enough first day," Slocum agreed, and waved good-bye to the man.

Slocum held Celia's saddle horse and waited for her to join them. Shorty took the boys and went to round up the cattle in the gray light with shafts of gold that streaked across the land.

She rushed out and took the reins. In a swift move she was in the saddle, and they herded the remuda out of the corral. Slocum felt relieved when they rode out under the gate pole. They were on their way to Ft. Robinson. The cattle were north of the ranch headquarters, and they would catch them shortly if Shorty and the two boys had managed to head them out. There was no extra help on this drive, though they could have used a few more riders.

"How's your brother going to get around?" Slocum asked as they trotted the horses after the gray mare with her bell in the lead.

"He says he will make it. Bruce is a tough individual, on himself and, I guess, others. I didn't realize the boys resented him that much, though."

"You can go back and care for him if he needs care," Slocum said. "We can manage these cattle and get them there."

She shook her head. "No. You'll need all the hands you have to get those steers up there. Bruce can take care of himself."

"Suits you, it suits me. You bring on the horses. I'll go help the boys."

"Yes sir—Boss."

He smiled at her mildly, then set the bay off in a long lope. He had lots of work to do.

Ten miles, he'd told Adolph, and they'd stop. He hoped he made it that far by dark with fresh cattle and all. This day would be a test for his new outfit. It sure was not overmanned.

9

The first day on the trail went smoothly. Too smoothly. Slocum felt uneasy, and he kept looking around for something to go wrong. Adolph proved his mettle and got along with the mules. His camp was set up along a stream and the fire going was a welcome sight. The German-accented man's apparent skills eased Slocum's concerns. He was obviously a professional.

Celia rode all day with Slocum, bringing the remuda along and handling the drag. He appreciated her horsemanship and grit. When they reached the campgrounds, she cut off from him to ride upstream for the willows to handle personal matters.

They had each ridden two good horses into the ground that day. Slocum roped out fresh ones for all of them to ride night guard on.

"I sure ain't complaining," Shorty said with a sigh, changing saddles to his fresh horse. "This day went well. And I got my fingers crossed we can keep on doing it like that all the way to Ft. Robinson."

Slocum agreed. He looked across the seat of his saddle at the herd scattered out grazing the brown grass. The fat steers proved easy to drive, and the quitters were not hard to convince that they had to stay in the herd.

"You know the weather's going to change," Shorty announced, grunting as he fought the latigo tight.

"Feels like the wind is coming from the northwest," Slocum agreed.

"I'd bet two bits that it's cold and snowing come daybreak."

"I won't bet with you." That was all Slocum needed. His cinch tight, he slapped down the stirrup and then studied the far-off cloud bank. "Not much we can do about that. We better get us some coffee and then relieve them boys so they can eat and get some rest."

He hitched his reins on the rope line stretched between two iron stakes, and walked over to the campground.

"You want some coffee, Boss Man?" Adolph asked, squatted down in his high-top lace-up boots by the fire.

"I'd take some. Guess Shorty would too. I'm fixing to ride out and send those two boys in. Feed them and send them to bed. They can do the second shift."

"You're sure not overloaded with workers," Adolph said, handing him a fresh cup.

"Nope. We could use some more help." Slocum blew on the surface of the tin cup, and the steam raced away in the fresh wind. Two more cowhands would have been great, but they had what they had. He could see one of the boys circling the cattle on his jaded horse. They were lucky these weren't fresh cattle out of the Brazos country, or they'd never have driven them this far; he'd had his share of those animals in the past.

"I'm glad for one thing." Adolph looked around from under the stiff brim of his four-peak hat to be certain they were alone. "Bruce. Glad he isn't with us." Then he poured Shorty's coffee.

"You and him have troubles?" Slocum asked.

"Oh, he is always mad about something. Two years ago, him and the hands got in a fistfight the second day out."

"He win?" Slocum looked in the man's blue eyes.

"No, she made them quit." Adolph nodded grimly as if reconsidering the matter. "They might have beat him up too."

"They got there all right? To Ft. Robinson?"

"Oh, yes, but it was all the time being on your guard. I just told him this was my camp. He could run the cattle and cowboys, but I would quit and walk home if he hollered at me like that one time."

"Your bluff work?"

Adolph grinned and nodded matter-of-factly. "He never hollered again."

"Finish that coffee and come on," Slocum said to Shorty as he downed the last of his own.

"Be right there."

"I'll send you a plate of food," the German offered.

"Fine, we'll be starved and appreciate it." Slocum grinned at the man and mounted up. He set out in a long lope for the boys.

With the two boys sent back for food and sleep, he and Shorty took up circling the spread-out herd. The clapper on the bell of the lead steer, a big brindle veteran of this drive, was wrapped in a rag to silence it. The steers began to lie down and chew their cuds as the low sun melted into the purple of the distant cloud bank.

Celia rode out to relieve one of them, but Slocum sent her and Shorty back. Shorty needed to eat his meal, and Slocum wanted her to get some rest—she looked tired. The cattle were doing fine and would need little tending for a while. Besides, the animals had finished sorting out herd seniority for the day. He felt they would soon all be lying down and the job of circling would ease up.

Shorty returned licking his lips. "Your turn."

"Food agree with you?"

"As good vittles as I've ate on the road. We need to hire him next time we make a drive."

"Thought you swore off cattle driving," Slocum said.

"I have. But I may need work again, and that Kraut is as good at his cooking as any I've tasted."

"I'll go see." Slocum booted his horse into a high lope for camp in the twilight.

Adolph filled his tin plate with rice, flour gravy, a couple of fried steaks, and some sourdough biscuits on the side. "I got stewed apples and raisins when you get that ate."

"Good," he said, and carried his supper to where Celia sat on the ground wrapped in a blanket against the sharp wind.

"Join me," she said with a smile, and tucked the blanket in tighter around her with her back to the chuck-wagon wheel. He nodded, and put his plate on the ground by her.

"Get my coffee and sweets and I will join you." He straightened, and went off.

"Plenty more," Adolph said.

"This will do me fine. I may fall asleep after eating all this."

"Them boys sure did." The man tossed his head toward the two in their bedrolls. Obviously they were fast asleep. They would need the rest. They'd not get much the next few weeks.

Slocum sat cross-legged and considered his food. He looked up with a frown at the sound of a voice above the wind.

"Hello the camp!" it called from the darkness.

"Boss Man, someone's coming," Adolph said, and jerked out a sawed-off shotgun from his box on the back of the chuck wagon.

"Who is it?" Celia asked softly as Slocum rose to his feet.

"Can't tell, they ain't on horseback."

"No?"

"Tell them to come on up," Slocum said to Adolph.

"Hey, don't shoot mister; we ain't outlaws," the shorter man said to Adolph as they came into the campfire's light.

They looked like Texas cowboys on foot. Slocum eased his hand off the gun butt as they dropped their bedrolls heavily on the ground.

"Injuns got our horses two days ago. Slipped up and took them while we slept. I'm Don Diggs and this is Melton Moore."

"Slocum's mine. That's Adolph and that's Miss Mc-Broom—she's the boss. You boys aim to walk back home?"

"No, sir. But we'd like to buy some grub and horses." They removed their hats and nodded politely at her.

"Ain't got any for sale. Adolph, fix them some food. You boys been on a drive?"

"Sure have. We took a herd to Standing Rock Reservation with Pete Tillman."

"I know Pete."

"You do? Well, Pete wanted us to ride a dang train home," the taller, stoop-shouldered one called Moore said. "I been wishing we had took the stinking train home ever since them Injun horse thieves got our ponies."

"We're short-handed," Slocum said as Celia joined them. "We're going to Ft. Robinson and then riding back to Texas ourselves. We could use the help."

"Mighty proud to meet you, ma'am," Diggs said for both of them with his hat in hand. "We ain't doing nothing but walking along. What do you say, Melton?"

"Beats walking."

"Fine," Slocum said, still bothered by their answers. But help was help. "There's some spare saddles in the chuck wagon. They ain't fancy rigs, but they'll do. You boys get plenty of rest tonight. Roll out at daybreak and we'll hit the trail."

"Thanks—Slocum," Diggs said, and Moore bobbed his head while taking his heaping plate from Adolph.

Seated back on the ground with Celia, Slocum started on his meal.

"That was a windfall, getting them," she whispered.

"Could be and couldn't be," he said between bites.

"You don't believe their story about Injuns getting their horses?" she asked in a whisper.

"They will do to watch."

"Why?"

He lowered his voice. "That Pete Tillman that he spoke about was laid up in San Antonio when I left. He had a broken leg."

"Then they lied?" she hissed.

"I'm not sure. Could be another Pete Tillman."

"Can we trust them?"

"Ain't got much choice. They'll bear watching." He listened to a wolf raise his throaty voice off in the distance. Time to get back to Shorty and the cattle.

"I'll get your dishes," she said, taking them and waiting for him to down his cold coffee.

"Keep your wits about you, girl."

"I will. You too."

He stared over at the two huddled cowboys facing the fire and stuffing themselves on Adolph's food. He hoped his hunch about them was wrong. But if they did one thing out of line, they'd wish the Injuns had killed them when they supposedly took their horses.

10

When they met on the far side of the herd, Slocum warned Shorty to keep an eye on the two new hands.

"What do you figure they're up to?" Shorty asked in the deep darkness of night as they reined up beside each other.

"They could have been in a scrape somewhere that they ain't talking about. They could work for rustlers who aim to take the herd, and they could be out and out liars."

"Why, hell, I went by and took Pete Tillman a bottle of good rye to get him through the pain before we left San Antone."

"I know you did. Keep it to yourself for now," Slocum said, and reined his horse about to head in the opposite direction around the dark herd. The clouds shut off the stars, and it was tough to even make out an outline of a resting steer. More than anything on such a dark night, he counted on the pony to know his way past the cattle. Slocum hummed out loud to keep his approach from spooking them.

Near to midnight, as close as Slocum could estimate, the Burns boys rode out from camp. Adolph's wind-up alarm clock had worked, he mused as he met them.

"Any trouble?" Barley asked.

"None at all. Ride around them and sing or talk out loud. It's darker than pitch out here, but the cattle have been quiet, so maybe they'll stay like that."

"We got two new hands?"

"Yeah."

"That will help."

"I hope so. You boys keep an eye on them two. They may be all right, and then they may have something up their sleeves."

"Adolph said Injuns got their horses while they were sleeping."

"Yeah, they said that. They came on foot anyway."

"You don't believe them?" Barley asked.

"We'll have to believe them for now. Keep what I said under your hats."

"We will."

"Good boys. See you at daybreak." He and Shorty rose in the stirrups and headed their horses for camp. They had all of four hours to sleep.

The two new cowboys were under their covers and appeared to be sound asleep. Slocum's head hit the saddle, his eyes locked shut, and he fell deep into slumber.

Celia's sleepy, hoarse voice awoke him. "Time to rise and shine, big man."

"What's it look like," he asked, sitting up, the cool dampness slapping his cheeks as he studied her smooth face in the fire's light.

"It may snow."

"Think you're right. Sleep good?" he asked her.

"Fair. It could have been better," she whispered, then shared a mischievous smile with him as she rose from her haunches. The waxed canvas duster's long tail whipped around her boots in the fresh wind.

"Fifteen more miles today and we only have ten days left to drive them," he said, throwing back his covers.

"I'll be glad and sad when we get there," she said quietly for him alone to hear.

"How's that?" he asked, sitting on top of his bedroll in the fresh predawn air and pulling on his boots. He'd kept them under the covers to keep them dry in case it snowed. The bad weather was close, but not there yet.

"I guess you'll ride on," she replied.

"Yeah, but you knew that."

She nodded and looked away. "There's a story there, isn't there? I mean, Slocum doesn't stay anywhere. Has no roots, for some reason."

"Not by choice, but no, I couldn't stay."

"You're the wind, no place to stop, no way to ever quit moving."

"Sums things up pretty well."

"I am glad that you came by. You showed me things about my life I was not looking at in the right perspective."

"That you should have a life of your own?"

She nodded.

"Good, because you should have one."

"I am going to try to do that." She hurried off to the campfire and busied herself helping Adolph.

His boots on, Slocum put on an extra shirt and then his jumper, buttoning it against the chill. The sky was cloudy, and it would be a late dawn. The way things were shaping up, he'd need more clothes before the day was over to stay warm. The precipitation, when it arrived, would probably start as slush, then turn to sleet, and then to snow.

After the morning meal, Slocum lined his crew up for their orders.

"Thad is the remuda man. You keep up with horses," Slocum announced after he introduced the new men. "Diggs, you and Moore ride right and left sides. Miss McBroom and I will bring up the drag. Shorty and Barley on point like they have been."

"I'll meet you at Honey Creek this afternoon," Adolph said, putting things up in the chuck box.

"We will try to get there before dark. Keep an eye out for renegades," Slocum warned him. He'd not spoken to the tall man about the two new hands, but the German was loyal enough that if he saw or heard anything amiss, he would act accordingly.

"I've got my pistols and this old shotgun in the chuck box," Adolph said. "They damn sure won't bother me much."

"Still, watch for them," Slocum said. They couldn't be careful enough.

Everyone saddled a fresh horse. Barley rushed around helping Adolph break camp and hitch the mules. Shorty went and undid the rag on the lead steer's bell. The clang of it brought the last of the cattle to their feet, and they started heading north with the cowboys hee-hawing them into a long rope like a train of railroad cars.

"Maybe you misjudged those two," Celia said as he boosted her in the saddle. "They're working fine out there."

"That ain't what I didn't like. They're rannies, all right, but they ain't told us everything else that they are."

"Whatever you say, Boss."

"Then get them drags going, girl," he said, and slapped her pony on the butt with his palm. She left in a lurch, never looking back as she rounded up the slowpokes.

"I may ride up ahead and look the country over this morning. You bring them horses slow and keep an eye on her for me," he said to Thad.

"Yes, sir."

"You have a gun?"

"We going to need one?" Thad asked, as if considering the notion.

"I can't say what you'd need it for, but I've got a loaded .30-caliber Colt in my saddlebags. You pack it in your bags, and without the caps on the nipples so it don't go off." He shared a serious look with the boy, then dug the revolver out. Forced to turn his hat into the sudden wind, he saved it from blowing off. "Just in case." He waved the small pistol at the boy.

"Yes, sir."

He handed him the revolver in the oily sheepskin case, and then the small tin of caps. "You used one before?"

"Yes, I can load and shoot it, don't worry, sir."

"Slocum."

"Slocum," the boy said. He waved the case and the tin at him, and then shoved them in his saddlebags. "I'll watch her good."

"Don't tell her either."

"I won't. I'm too bashful anyway." The youth had a blush on his face as he laughed.

Slocum watched Adolph roll off in a rattle of wheels with his fresh mules. Slocum studied the chuck wagon's tailgate as it headed out around the herd and north. Things were lined up for the day despite the overcast and threatened snow.

If those two hands had cohorts, then they might be camped not far away. Slocum decided to do some checking on his own. If he could stop something from happening early enough before it happened, they might make it to Ft. Robinson unscathed.

"You make it by yourself for a few hours?" he asked Celia, riding in close.

"Sure, I'll be fine. Where are you going?"

"To check on our neighbors, if we have any."

"Go ahead. I can handle this drag business. But you be careful out there, Slocum." She frowned and tightened the rawhide string under her chin that held her hat on. "There are renegade bands all over this country."

"I know, and I will be careful."

He short-loped the bay northeasterly. It was the direction his new hands had come from. He crossed the brown-grass bowl, and on the rise he could look back and see the long line of cattle snaking its way northward. In a few miles he found a creek and discovered fresh horse tracks. As he'd suspected, there were no boot tracks in the soft ground where two men had crossed the stream on foot. The shod horse prints led easterly. They had been planted close by just as he'd thought.

How many were with the main bunch? Two riders had obviously led the two riderless horses back toward their camp, wherever it was located. That was simple enough to read in the soft ground. Diggs and Moore hadn't walked over a mile to get to the cattle camp. They hadn't been anywhere near foot-sore enough for men supposed to have walked two days in pointed-toed boots with slant heels made for riding. Slocum knew that in gravel-cactus country like the Arizona desert, leather soles wore out in a day or less of walking.

He topped another rise, and smelled campfire smoke. It was on the wind. Indians didn't let such smells escape often. More than likely it was from a white man's fire. He booted the bay northward, and the first flakes of snow began to fall.

11

No need to take chances stumbling into their camp. Slocum decided to approach it on foot. He hobbled his horse in the coulee. Dollar-sized flakes swirled around him. Whoever was camped under those cottonwoods over the rise didn't need to know that he was coming to check on them. This snow would hide a lot. It would also make it hard for him to find his way back to the herd again. But he shrugged away his concern; the storm wouldn't last forever. He straightened, satisfied that the hobbled pony would be there when he returned.

A cold flake melted on his cheek when he removed the Winchester from the scabbard and moved up the hillside. How close would he have to get to learn who was in the camp? In this weather, dang close. He turned up the collar on his jumper, and icy drips ran down his neck. With the Winchester in his gloved hand, he wondered how Shorty and the crew were making it. He hoped they weren't too separated from Adolph and had made camp at the onset of the storm. Obviously, from the tracks leading him to this place, this bunch was connected to the two cowboys Diggs and Moore. This was obviously not a church meeting.

He came on a low run to use the cover of a topless wagon that was this side of their camp. In the swirling dark world, he had made out the ash bows sticking up. In a flash, he ducked under the wagon bed, squatted on his boot heels, and studied the camp. Woodsmoke on the wind was strong in his nose.

"When we taking that herd?" someone asked, standing at the roaring fire. At the distance and with the snow's fury, he could tell little about the man. Slocum turned his ear and listened.

"About five days. We'll let them drive closer to Ft. Robinson. Then we'll swoop in and do it."

"Poor old Diggs and Moore out there working in this—"

"Hell, they'll get their share."

Huddled under the wagon bed on his haunches, the rifle in his hand, Slocum figured that he'd heard enough. The two men were talking not ten yards away and warming their hands at the blazing fire, which he envied so much. At least he knew what was happening. How many others were there in this group besides the two hands with the herd? How would he handle the ones in the camp? There had to be several more rannies out of his sight in the two tents he could see if they were taking over the herd.

He wondered what he should do next, then decided to get back and expose those boys' hands before Celia got hurt in the middle of all this. He turned on his stiff boot soles and started out from under the wagon.

"Who the hell is that out there?" one of them shouted. "Stop!" Too late. He'd been spotted. Slocum began to run, cursing his luck. No time to do anything else.

"Injuns!" the other shouted.

The blast of their pistols was loud. Slocum knew he was struck in the back. The sharp, hot slap felt like a bad bee sting, and it doubled his speed into the arms of the snowstorm. If they thought there were more "Indians" with him, they might not dare come out of the camp after him. It was his only hope to reach his horse. At the crest of the coulee, he realized that somewhere he'd dropped his rifle. No time for that now. He staggered downhill in the deepening snow until he made out the shape of his mount. He glanced backwards—nothing but swirling snowflakes. He removed his skinning knife from the sheath behind his back as he half ran to the cow pony. He dropped down and slashed the rope hobbles.

He had to get back to the herd and warn Shorty and Celia. Two tries, and then he was in the saddle and headed out of the draw. Hot sticky blood oozed under his shirt, and then glued the material to his back. Fresh wet flakes exploded and swirled before him in blinding waves. He'd be lucky to ever find the herd in this storm. He pushed the horse. Pursuit was not the thing worrying him the most. Celia's safety and that of the others worried him more than anything.

The wound in his shoulder felt as if they had hurled a huge lance into his back and the long shaft was wobbling from it as he rode, which caused him to grit his teeth. His good hand clinched the saddlehorn as snowflakes melted on the skin. He tried to keep his vision straight. This would be a long day. A very long day.

Somewhere, hours later, he fainted and fell from the horse. Time escaped him, but it was still daylight when he awoke face-down in the snow. He rose with much effort. The cold shot through his body as he protected his right side and used his left hand to push off. The horse wouldn't be far, it would ground-tie, but he couldn't see far in the snow's blinding fury. He went twenty paces in one direction—no horse. Then he went back on his tracks, and went a quarter turn the next way the same distance. Still no horse. He returned to the center of his pivot and tried it again. When he had been all the way around the wheel without any luck, he repeated his steps, only he went twice as far out this time.

His brain was numb and he couldn't shake it clear. How much blood had he lost? No telling. Again he continued his wagon-wheel search. It was on the third spoke that he spotted the horse standing hip-shot, butt to the wind.

Thank God. Slocum would rope himself in this time. The horse's instinct might take him back to the others. A shiver ran up his spine as he shoved his left boot in the stirrup, and then pulled himself up with a hard-fought effort.

"Go home, horse," he said, and gave him his head.

Then he tied himself in the saddle with his lariat so if he passed out again, he wouldn't fall off. The soft white feathers danced around him and he closed his eyes. His chances of ever finding the others grew dimmer and dimmer.

It was nighttime—dark, still snowing—when he awoke with a start. Still roped in. He felt grateful for that. The deep fiery pain in his shoulder throbbed. Where was he? His horse was among some other horses. Slocum tried to see in the night. He blinked at their fuzzy forms. Then his heart stopped. The one close to him bore the notched ears of a buffalo horse. His pony had brought him to an Indian camp. He looked around. Then, out of nowhere, he heard the war cries, and before he could boot his mount away, someone was on his back trying to tear him from the saddle. He undid the rope in a quick twist, and then tried to get a hold on his attacker.

They fell from the horse, wrestling, the pain in his upper body shattering his brain. He and the warrior were struggling in the snow. Other Indians came to help the buck, and Slocum soon found himself pinned on his back on a drift. The cold penetrated his body, and he realized that his time left in this world would be short.

Then a torch was held up, and he could see the angry glares of a half-dozen copper faces peering at him. His last struggles would be useless. How would he die, by knife or hatchet?

"No!" someone shouted.

He blinked at the swirl of her buckskin-fringe skirt as a woman came forward and stepped over him. Her guttural Sioux was loud and demanding. The men's angry replies matched her fury.

Feather almost stepped on him. She roughly shoved away the boy holding his left arm. They had fierce words and for a moment, Slocum wondered if they would fight over the matter. The young boy was on his feet in an instant, but slunk away from her wrath.

She told the other one—the one who had dragged him from the horse—to move away in Sioux. Slocum could see the harshness in his face. The warrior was older than the others, and was not ready to give up his hold on this intruder no matter what she said or threatened him with.

The buck reached out and struck Slocum with his open hand on the chest, hard enough to draw up a cough that hurt.

His action drew a swift moccasin kick from her that sent the buck sprawling away. She charged after him as their words grew more heated.

Slocum hoped she didn't go too far away, for the others were still there in the torchlight, ready to pounce on him should she lose the argument. In a minute, her face black with rage, she came stomping back, jerked Slocum to his feet with her right hand, and glared off in the darkness, shouting Sioux obscenities at the other buck.

"Come with me," she said, turning and starting off.

"Yes, ma'am," Slocum said, and quickly followed in her footsteps.

A woman under a buffalo robe spoke to her as they passed and Feather turned to him with a concerned look on her face.

"Are you bleeding?" she asked.

"Yes, but you can look at it later," he said, anxious to go to her place and get away from the angry scrutiny of the warriors, even if they were hardly more than boys. He waved her on.

She bent over to enter a lodge, motioned for him to come inside, and held the skin back for him. He looked around at the snarling camp dogs and the dark eyes that shone in the night, suspicious eyes that studied him. Then he bent over and entered the tepee. On his knees, he half crawled to the fire ring. There he straightened up and sat back on his legs, the heat from the small fire warming the tingling skin on his face. It felt heavenly.

She knelt beside him, removed his jumper, and then unbuttoned his shirt as if he were unable to. Her looks of disapproval and head-shaking continued. With care she pulled the blood-stuck material from his back.

"You lay down."

He obeyed, and stretched out on the buffalo hide. Small drafts of chilly air swept the tepee floor as she washed his wound with an icy rag and equally cold water; then he felt her scrub the dried blood from his back.

"That bullet must come out," she said, probing her finger in the wound. The jabs were blinding, and he gritted his teeth.

"Yes," he managed.

"I will go borrow a tool."

He nodded that he'd heard her. With the sharp animal smell of the tanned hide in his nose, he felt her cover him with a blanket and he mumbled thanks, but her soft moccasin soles were already at the doorway. Slocum closed his eyes. What kind of tool?

She returned and showed him the screw on the end of a ramrod used to remove bullets from a gun barrel. He shook his head and hoped the bullet wasn't in so deep that she needed the whole rod. Her efforts were clumsy to him, but it was so hard to hold the long rod up and engage the screw in the bullet lodged in his back. He caught himself screaming, and then clamped his mouth shut until he lost consciousness.

"Here," she said when he awoke. In his fogged vision he saw the flattened lead poised on the end of the screw.

"Yes," he agreed, and tried to shut his eyes to the deep pain that engulfed his entire shoulder.

"I burned it out with gunpowder," she said, and held a pottery cup up to his lips, holding his head up for him to drink it.

He nodded. That was what he'd smelled, burnt gunpowder, before he'd passed out the last time. Slowly he raised up and sipped on whatever she had for him to drink.

"Willow-bark tea. It will help you heal," she announced. "I have packed the wound with leaves of many healing plants."

"Yes," he said in gratitude. Only time would tell. Had it quit snowing? He neither knew the day nor the time. The orange light of the small fire in the center shone on her long copper cheekbones. In her large brown eyes, he saw her concern. He was on his own now. She'd done all she could.

"If I die, there's some money, a little, in my pockets, and you may have the horse too," he said.

She shook her head. "I have talked to Sho-tow. She says you will live to ride away."

"Witch, huh?"

"Yes, but she knows the signs."

The tea was helping. The worst of the pain was dying

down. Someone once said that even the pain lessened before one went over the big divide. Slocum closed his eyes. The lids were too heavy to keep open, and he soon fell deep asleep, unsure he would ever wake up from this nap.

Several hours later, he awoke. A pressing on his bladder had awakened him. She was seated close by him cross-legged, busy sewing on a buckskin garment. The material she worked on hid a portion of her shapely brown legs as she paused to listen to him.

"I need to go outside," he said.

She nodded that she understood. "I will help."

"A man too weak to go out and piss on his own ain't worth much," he mumbled as she helped him to his feet. He discovered she had removed his boots, but the effort to put them on was too much to even consider. He would go outside in his stocking feet. With her assistance and support, he managed to make it into the night. The sharp screeching north wind stung his face, and they only went around the tepee a portion of the way. His stocking feet broke through the crust into the powdery snow beneath it. There, in the lee side of the structure away from some of the sharp wind, he undid his pants and, feeling self-conscious when he began, at last found relief in a high arch.

Finished, he replaced the buttons and with her support, turned and started for the opening. Nothing stirred around the half-dozen tepees except the sharp ice that the wind bore. How were Shorty and Celia making out? He had to get them word about the ambush that those outlaws planned for them.

With toes about to cramp from the cold, he felt relieved to be back in the security of the tepee and on the dry buffalo-hide rugs. His strength was drained from the short trip, and he sat up and drank the lukewarm tea she served him, and then dropped to the blankets. In moments he was asleep. He felt her cover him up before falling off.

He dreamed of war battles. Exploding shells blowing men's bodies asunder. The acrid eye-tearing stench of spent black powder smoke burning out the lining of his nostrils and eyes. No end to the death and dying around him, yet nary a ball struck him in two days of fierce fighting. His comrades fell like tenpins all around him. He could save nary a one. He tried to drag one man he knew from behind a fence, but the man died in his arms. Nothing he did turned out right.

Then he became warm and he felt himself smile. It was not the sun that warmed him, but the luscious naked body of Feather.

"You were shivering and cold," she said, pushing the hair back from his forehead. "You were saying, 'kill them blue-bellies.' "

"I was dreaming."

She scooted closer, her long tight breasts and warm hard stomach pressed to him, and he closed his eyes. Still shivering, he forgot about the cold and savored her closeness. His concern for Shorty and Celia returned, but it soon left too. All things earthly escaped his numb mind, and he closed his eyes and slept.

12

"Where in the hell do you reckon Slocum is?" Shorty rubbed his bristle-edged mouth with his palm and scowled at the snowy sea that stretched for miles. Shorty Giles had spent the first thirty-four years of his life figuring out how to get out of work. This morning, as the frigid north wind swept his face and drove the chill of cold through his layers of clothing, he felt the yoke of responsibility that had settled heavily on his shoulders, and he wasn't comfortable with the new position.

"He may be laying up until the storm passes," Diggs said.

"No, he's done enough scouting, he'd of come back by now."

"Want us to go look for him?"

Shorty shook his head. "No, he wouldn't want or expect that. He'd expect us to get these cattle to Ft. Robinson. That'll be our job until we get it finished."

"But what if—" Celia cut off her words of concern and bit her lower lip. Then she blurted out, "He could be hurt out there and need us."

"Slocum would want us to keep moving this herd. Snow's stopped. Maybe it's blown away ahead and they can find some graze. Diggs, you ride point with Barley today." Shorty wished he had better plans than simply heading northwest, but he didn't for the moment. From the corner of his eye, he could see Diggs saying something to the stoop-shouldered Moore. If they were in cahoots over something, there was nothing he could do about it for the time being but bluff his way along until Slocum got back. He needed both of them to move the herd.

The cowboys strung out the steers. Shorty, Thad, and Celia helped Adolph harness the team.

"No need in hurrying," Shorty said to the cook. "You find water or a place clear enough of snow to let them graze, we'll stop even if it's only midday."

"I understand. You figure Indians got Slocum?" Adolph asked with a vexed-looking frown.

"Maybe wild horses. He ain't one to quit. Something happened, and since the snow's stopped, he might come riding up any time. I'm doing what he'd do, getting things moving. We need to keep moving." He turned to Celia and almost swallowed his tongue. He didn't ever speak much to women in her class, and he found words difficult. "Ma'am, you might ought to bundle up and ride with Adolph today. It must be zero out here, I don't—"

"Don't worry about me, Shorty. I can ride drag."

"But it don't seem right," he protested. Somehow he wanted to protect her, and felt distracted he couldn't do more to insure her safety. What would Slocum do? Hell, he'd take charge, but Shorty wasn't Slocum either.

"I'll be fine. You did well. Just keep things going until—until Slocum gets back," she said, mounting up.

"Yes, ma'am, I'll sure try."

He had every intention of doing that—keeping things moving. With a hard knot lodged behind his tongue making it difficult to swallow, Shorty searched the snowy sea and saw nothing coming from the direction Slocum had ridden off in, or from the south either. Oh, he'd come back. Slocum was no quitter. Shorty drew a deep breath of the cold air for strength, and then he mounted up. Celia had already taken up driving the stragglers after the herd. The operation was on the move and he was in charge.

At mid-afternoon, they came to a running creek, his outriders swung the herd into a bow so they would be spread out to drink, and Shorty waved at Adolph, who was set up on the far bank. Grateful the man knew his business, Shorty forded the branch to be satisfied that the snow wasn't too deep for the cattle to paw through. It looked satisfactory, and he swung back to the chuck wagon and dismounted. This business of being boss had his stomach tied in knots.

"Coffee?" the German asked.

"Yes, sir," Shorty said.

"Snow's not deep here." Adolph scuffed it back with the sole on his lace-up boot.

"It's a good place," Shorty agreed as the others rode in. "Them longhorns have been up here a winter. They can find that grass."

"Coffee," Barley said, and with a grin at the prospect of it, bailed off his horse.

Shorty nodded, and went to where Celia had dismounted.

"You're not frozen, are you?"

She looked into his eyes and forced a small smile at his concern. "No, I'm fine. Did we come ten miles today?"

"Close to it, I figured. They get some water and they'll paw up some snow and graze out here. That will keep part of the fat on them."

"Fine. You're as concerned about him as I am, aren't you?" she asked in a low voice.

"I been looking all day expecting him to ride in. This isn't like him."

"Something's gone wrong, but we may never know."

"Right, ma'am."

"Shorty, call me Celia, please."

"Yes, I will. Celia. Get some coffee, it'll warm you some."

"I may never be warm again."

"I know the feeling." He grinned at her, feeling at once more comfortable in her company.

She turned and squinted against the glare down their back-trail. He ain't out there, Shorty wanted to tell her aloud. I've looked for him too until my danged eyes are sore.

She shook her head disappointed, and headed for Adolph, who was bringing her a cup of steaming coffee. The boys were crowded around the campfire trying to warm up. Shorty felt relieved that the cattle were spreading out and pawing up snow for the feed under it. Things were in hand.

The fresh new wind struck his face as Shorty considered his own coffee. He sighed at his discovery. It might feel cold now, but the new wind would soon warm things up. Warmer weather came on the wings of an old south wind, a breeze off the warm Texas country far, far away. It would soon melt this white mess and he could get on with the drive.

"What's the matter?" she asked, bringing her cup over.

"Wind's coming out of the south. Feel it? Going to warm up."

"Yes. It's too early to stay this cold for long."

"Good. We can start making that fifteen miles a day that Slocum promised you."

"Shorty, we can camp here for a day if you want to go look for him."

"Be a lot of country to look over, but I could—no, ma'am. I mean, Celia." He looked around and then lowered his voice. "Them two new hands that he hired still make me uneasy. Slocum caught them in one lie, and I don't trust them well enough to leave you here with them."

"I can fend for myself."

"No. Slocum would say for us to keep going. He might be beyond our help. He's a big boy and he can handle himself if he ain't gone to his reward."

"You think that's best? Going on?"

"I know it is, ma—Celia."

"Fine, you're the boss."

"Boys," Shorty called out to the others. "No need to ride out for a spell, those cattle are doing fine. Warm your feet and fingers at the fire. Drink some more coffee and warm up some here. It's going to be a long night to ride guard."

"Thanks," one of them said.

Shorty watched the smiles on their faces. They were haggard enough. Those longhorns weren't going anywhere. He needed to save his horseflesh and his riders.

"Where are you going?" Celia asked as he mounted up.

"I seen some deadwood I can drag in for Adolph, and then I may ride a ways east and look around."

"I'll go rope that snag for him. You go look a little." She waved toward the east.

"I'll do that."

"You be careful," she said.

He eyed the two new hands, who were busy drinking coffee and talking with the others. They looked harmless enough for the moment. "I will."

He exchanged a private smile with her. Shorty sent his pony into a long lope. It was sure different working for a woman that attractive. He'd known his share of "working women." Even asked one to marry him once, but it didn't work out and he had not regretted it, seeing some of his old pards knuckled down to small outfits or even farming. Still, Celia McBroom made his guts roil at the notion of her fine figure. Lots of woman there.

There was not much to see but more snow, but maybe from a high place he could spot Slocum's horse. He couldn't be sure. He booted the cow pony up the grade. At least this way he could say he'd looked for him.

Shorty crossed the first rise and decided that since nothing showed, he'd try one more. He had a few hours until dark, and there would be stars in the clear sky to guide him back to camp if it was later.

A coyote crossed to the south, keeping a parallel course with him. Then he saw them. Riders—they were hatless. Indians, a handful of bucks on horses. He whirled the pony around and headed down his back tracks in a fury of dry snow powder.

The unmistakable yips of the braves discovering him forced him to lash the horse with his reins. He had to get back to camp and hope they were ready for this bunch. Those bucks, a half mile behind him, wanted blood and a scalp lock, and he had no intention of giving them his. He leaned over the horse's neck as the saddle leather complained and the pony churned up snow that swept his chin.

Had those bloodthirsty bastards got ten Slocum? There were close to six of them by his quick count, and they might have. Their war cries carried on the wind. One more rise to climb, then he'd be in sight of the cow camp and would signal with a gunshot for the others to be ready.

The Indians fired at him. The dull sounds of their shots shattered the air louder than the hard breathing of his horse. His pony's breath was raging in and out of his lungs and great grunts of effort escaped his nose. *Don't quit me. They eat fat ponies.* He leaned over the horse's neck to make a lesser target and help his stride.

He crossed the ridge and drew out his .44. He turned back and took two quick snap shots at his pursuers. In the distance, he could see the others at camp, taking Winchesters out of the chuck wagon. Good, they would greet these renegades with some hot lead.

He slid to a halt at the wagon, dismounted, and drew out his long gun from the scabbard.

"Guess who's coming for supper," he said, joining the others spread out on the ground on their bedrolls.

"Where did you find them?" Barley asked.

"Oh, across the ridge."

"You reckon they got Slocum?"

"Better ask them. Hold your fire, boys, until they get closer."

"Any sign of him?" Celia asked from the bedroll to the right of the youth.

Shorty shook his head. "No sign. I ran into that bunch is all."

"What are they doing out there now?" Barley asked as the Indians checked their charge and milled around on their horses.

"Having a parley," Shorty said. "Working up their nerve to rush us or not."

"We ain't got long to wait," Diggs said, and six abreast the renegades came screaming at the tops of their lungs and firing at them. A stray bullet struck a metal tub on the side of the chuck wagon with a loud clang and drew a curse from Adolph.

"I just got that retinned, you worthless red devils!" He raised up on his knees and began to shoot his rifle off-handed at them. Two of his shots took hold. One downed a painted pony in a snowy crash; the other sent a rider off the tail of his horse.

The renegades, hanging low on their horses, went screaming off to the east. The horseless brave got to his feet and ran as fast as his fringed legs would carry him out of rifle range.

"Will they quit?" Celia asked.

"Not yet," Shorty said, his stomach in a hard knot. There could be many more of them out there, or these could be the only ones. There was no way to know, but they probably wouldn't give up this easy. There was food and supplies in the chuck wagon, and their horses, all things a buck needed in an early, snowy winter.

Shorty closed his eyes. Slocum needed to be there. He'd driven big herds to Kansas. Slocum had messed with Indians and rustlers—hell, all Shorty could recall was one old chief wanting some beef, and the trail boss cutting him out four sore-footed steers that everyone hated because they couldn't keep up. These bloody devils wanted more than a few foot-sore steers—they wanted to count coup.

He rose to his knees to see if he could make out what they were going to do next. Damn, what a mess.

13

"Slo-cum," she whispered, raised on her elbow and leaning over him.

He opened his matted eyes and stared into hers. Still groggy and reminded how badly his shoulder hurt, he forced a smile at her closeness. The tepee was dark, and he could barely make out her face.

"The others are gone," she said in a low husky voice.

What time of day was it? How long had he been there in her care? Then there was the problem of the herd, the snow, and those outlaws. He had to get back. The truth was he hardly had the strength to move. What did she mean by "the others"? The rest of the Sioux in camp had left?

"I need to get to my people," he said in a dry voice that shocked him with its rasping sound. "They will have much trouble."

She shook her head in disapproval, and swept back the hair from his face with her cool palm. "You could hardly sit on a horse."

"I have to. Have to find them." He closed his eyes, and her rich musk wafted up his nose and the radiant heat of her naked body made him comfortably warm under the covers.

"They are in the direction the sun sets?" she asked.

"Yes."

"I will fix a travois to carry you."

"I can ride."

"And fall from your horse?" She shook her head in disapproval, and propped herself up on her elbow to look him in his face.

"I have to get stronger," he said, and drew a deep breath. He studied her full deep-brown copper lips only inches away from him. They looked so inviting, so tempting.

"Where did the others go?" he asked.

"To look for meat."

He nodded. There was little left for them to hunt but cattle in this country. He hadn't seen but a few buffalos since they began the drive, and *they* were scattered. Nothing like the times before when he crossed this country and the buffalo herds went by for days.

"How long have they been gone?"

"The women left this morning to follow the men."

"I think I can ride."

"I will take you to this herd."

"Good. Feather?"

"Yes?"

"There are some bad white men camped south of here. I think south of here. They shot me and will try to take the herd from the woman who owns it."

He felt her palm slither over the corded muscles of his stomach. Then she closed her eyes, and he pulled her face to his with his good arm. At his first taste of her lips, they were unmoved and pursed, but when her exploring fingers encircled his rising manhood, her petals parted and his tongue reached the honey of her mouth. The rising tide of sweetness and newfound urgency consumed their contact.

She slipped around to straddle his legs, and dragged her hard nipples across his chest as she moved upward. Then, on top of his hips, she raised up, and the rush of cold air swept over them as she inserted him in her wet opening. Then she settled on top of him, pulling the covers up over her back.

"Lay still," she whispered, and began to work her hips against him. With the grinding motion, she began to receive more and more of him each time.

His shoulder ached, but the heady power of her passion

swept most of that away. They kissed and she worked on top of him—harder and harder. He raised his hips up to meet her as her walls began to contract on him and he fought for more. Her long firm breasts swung in her fury, until he finally caught one and began to kiss the end. She cried out aloud and moved for him to take more of it.

Then a low moan escaped her as she arched her back and straightened in a deep trance. He felt the warm flush of fluids as she braced herself to keep from crushing him. Her brown eyes swarmed, and she disengaged herself to lay beside him. His eyelids closed and he slept.

The travois poles hissed in the snow when he awoke. The bright snow blinded him. She had put his pistol in his lap under the blankets. He felt jarred and stiff on the litter, but he kept passing out and coming to. There was no way in his condition that he could ride a horse very far.

His vision of the white landscape behind them was all he could see. Could she see the herd?

"See them?" he called out to her as she rode the travois horse.

"No, I have seen nothing."

"We should cross their tracks somewhere out here."

"I will know the tracks of many cattle."

"I wasn't—" He drew a deep breath. She knew what she was doing. Why couldn't he be quiet? Still, he wondered about the safety of Celia and his crew. It was a damn fool thing getting shot spying on those rannies. He should have rushed in and killed the whole damn bunch and ended it. But murdering wasn't his way. Still, Shorty, the two boys and Celia had two men not to be trusted in their midst. Big mess. He closed his eyes at the throbbing. He must have lost lots of blood to be this weak.

He awoke and studied the noontime sun. Damn, he couldn't keep his eyes open long enough to do anything. No way he'd ever hold off those rustlers in this shape. He'd be as valuable as nothing to his friends. Still, if he was there and could help them somehow . . . Slocum fell back into his groggy sleep.

"I thought you needed to stand up," she said, undoing the blankets over him.

He rose, blinking his eyes at the glare. The fresh south wind struck him and sent cold through his clothing. She stepped in and assisted him.

"Yes, I'll be fine," he said, feeling his legs straighten under him. He needed to walk around some. Gazing around, he was disappointed to see nothing. Nebraska was a big country, lots of wide-open land. That herd would be like a needle in a haystack to find, but they did leave tracks. How far had he wandered on his horse after being shot? No telling.

"I want to ride double with you," he said.

"Fine," she said, gathering the lead to her small blue roan that carried her packs and holding the bay horse's reins in the other hand.

She mounted, and then he swung up behind her with some effort. His arms encircled her, and they started off again. He felt better riding double than lying on the travois. If he could keep awake, that would be even better. His eyelids felt laced with lead weights.

By late afternoon the sun and south wind had begun to warm the air, and the snow turned to mush. He tried to shake the dizziness that kept making him groggy, but to no avail. At last, he had her stop under the pretext of emptying his bladder. His efforts to stay awake proved to be impossible, and she herded him back to his pallet on the travois.

"I thought you would fall off before you gave up," she said as she hurried about, covering him with blankets and robes.

"I—" He sighed in defeat. "Hope we find them."

"We will," she said, and ran to mount up.

He only wished he shared her faith. They needed to find the herd. With his head on the pillow made from a buffalo-calf skin, he let himself slip off into a drugged sleep as the poles hissed through the melting snow and gave him a shaky ride.

At nightfall, she made camp and cut cedar boughs from the hillside for a dry bed for them to lie upon. The temperature had risen unbelievably with the south wind, and besides being warmer, he felt stronger. He watched the horses finding grass easily under the mushy crust. They barely pawed, submerging their muzzles in it, snatching out great bunches of fodder in their mouths.

He worried that he might have ridden past the herd's tracks during the time when he had been wounded and so disoriented. Feather knew nothing of the outlaws' camp. There was just too much country.

"Are you hungry?" she asked, returning with her arms loaded with boughs.

"I can eat. Why?"

"Eating will make you strong," she said, piling the pungent boughs up for their bed.

"Finding that herd will make me feel better."

She raised to her full height. "This woman with the cattle—she is your woman?"

"No." He shook his head. "This woman has a brother who she belongs to."

Feather stopped arranging her cedar branches and blinked at him in disbelief. "Really?"

"Unfortunately, yes. She is not my woman. But she is a good person. You would like her."

"Her brother protects her?" Feather nodded as if that answered her concern.

"No. They live as man and wife."

"How could they?"

"I can't explain it. It happened, and they live away from other people." He shrugged. "Indians do strange things too."

"Yes. Tomorrow we will find your herd."

"Are you a witch now who can see the future?" he asked.

"No. But you will see."

"I believe you," he said, and under her disapproving look began to transfer some of the hides to the new bed of boughs.

"I will do that," she said sharply.

"No, this lazy white man who slept all day will." His back turned to her, he winced when his actions caused his sore shoulder to catch. With the next thick robes from the pile, he took more pains to carry them from the travois to the bed and not toss them.

14

Shorty wondered if the bucks had had enough, or simply gone over the hill to get charged up to come back again. They had ridden down warily and picked up their wounded warrior. Then, without a war cry, they had ridden off to the east and across the crest.

"You figure they're out there making more medicine?" Diggs asked.

"I ain't sure of nothing," Shorty said. "But we're fixing a rope corral for the horses for tonight to keep them up close, and someone needs to guard it. Them bucks would rather steal a horse as eat. If we lose them, we're in big trouble."

"Between riding herd and guarding horses, we ain't getting much sleep tonight," Moore grumbled.

"I'd rather have my hair than be planted out here," Shorty said, cutting a hard look at the man. Moore was one of those natural complainers. Nothing ever suited him, and for the moment that had worn thin.

"Yeah, guess you're right." Moore ducked his head and started off.

"No guess to it. Thad, you and Moore take the first shift. Diggs and Barley the second one. I'll look about the horses tonight."

"I can do one shift," Celia said.

Shorty nodded that he'd heard her. No way would he allow

her to be exposed to danger. Besides, he didn't want her sitting up all night—it wasn't right, and he had enough problems being short-handed. Those two Texas rannies hadn't done anything out of line, but he watched them closely. If they planned to steal the herd, they would probably do it closer to Ft. Robinson. If they had help nearby, he'd not seen a sign of them—nor of Slocum, and that bothered him worse than anything. It had been over two days since Slocum had ridden out.

At the moment, Shorty wanted a stiff drink of whiskey. He should have told Slocum to do this drive by himself and ridden back to Texas, where it was warm and dry, instead of standing in his wet cold boots in this melting sloop worrying about everything that could go wrong.

"You're doing a good job of managing things," Celia said to him quietly.

Jarred from his thoughts, he nodded woodenly at her words of encouragement, and stared across the white patches on the brown grass. He needed to find Slocum. Maybe the man was dead, no telling. But Shorty had to keep his guard up. All looking for Slocum had brought so far were some bloodthirsty bucks ready to pounce on his herd.

At nightfall, he stood with his back to the chuck wagon. He'd made several rounds of the camp and horse herd with the rifle in the crook of his arm. They were camped on a large flat, and no buck could creep up on them unseen in the starlight. The cattle were across the small creek, and he could hear the riders talking and singing as they rode around the herd. Every little while, a wolf gave a throaty howl at the sliver of a moon. The warmer air felt better as he stepped out again to make his round.

Texas Comanches he knew more about. He'd ridden on raids against them. Had been attacked a few times by small war parties that struck at cow camps he worked out of. They'd been fierce raiders that stormed screaming upon them. He had been lucky thus far in his life. But how would Sioux attack? The unknown was what made his gut curdle as he slipped along in the darkness.

He paused and looked hard across the night-shrouded landscape. Did something move out there? If he shot, would it stampede the herd? Slowly, in deep concentration, he drew a deep breath and studied the inky land for a sign of movement. The hair rose on the back of his neck. Why did he think the Indians were out there? Why did he imagine they were creeping in closer by the hour on him and the camp? Or was it *only* his imagination?

He walked around the horses, who were grunting and shuffling their hooves on the mushy ground in their sleep. Grateful for the stake-rope trap, he returned to the wagon without seeing a thing. That didn't mean there weren't any Indians out there, only that they weren't showing themselves—yet.

What should he do? Being boss had become a lot tougher than he had ever imagined.

What he wasn't seeing out there was what worried him more than anything else. He couldn't let Celia stand this guard. If anything happened to her, it would be his fault and he would never forgive himself. Maybe she would sleep through the guard change. He could wish she would anyway.

The alarm clock ringing on the chuck wagon tailgate made him jump. He moved quickly to turn it off. Adolph was up from his bedroll and stirring the fire to heat up the coffee for the waking boys to drink before they rode out and replaced the others. To Shorty's dismay, she was getting up too and putting on her boots.

The Burns boys and Moore came in, and they dropped heavily from their saddles.

"Seen anything?" Shorty asked.

"Coyote or two is all. Maybe they gave up," Barley said.

"Don't count on it. Get some sleep," he said to them.

"You do the same," she said under her breath, nudging him with her elbow.

"I will."

"No, now."

"Yes, ma'am." He set the rifle down by the wagon wheel. Adolph was already back under the covers. It hadn't taken him long to get back to sleep. Shorty drew the blankets over himself. No need to undress—he might have to jump up any minute.

His sleep was troubled, and he awoke several times, listening to the night sounds and seeing her by the wagon holding the rifle. Then he went back to his slumber.

He rose before the purple edge of dawn creased the eastern horizon. Adolph nodded and poured him a cup of fresh coffee. She was squatted on her heels with the rifle over her lap when Shorty joined her.

"See anything?" he asked, trying to see against the last wall of night.

"No, but I thought I heard horses out there a little while ago."

Her words struck him like a slap. *Sounds of horses.* That was all they'd heard before the Comanches attacked them that morning west of the Pecos. Damn, the Indians must be close; but a woman had keener ears than a man. He needed to get things ready for the attack, and quick.

"Ring that triangle, Adolph! Get them boys in here from the herd! Everyone up, hurry!"

"What's wrong, Shorty?" she asked, looking bewildered.

"They're going to charge us when the sun is in our eyes. We've got to be ready. You heard horses, all right, just over the hill. You never can hear the damn Injuns. You may have saved our hides."

"What's wrong?" Moore asked, staggering around half asleep in the fire light.

"Renegades are going to charge us."

"How do you know?" He reared back and blinked at Shorty.

"Damnit, I still got my hair, ain't I? Get your rifle and shells, get under that wagon. You too," he said to her.

"Where you want me?" Barley asked.

"On that side."

"What's wrong?" Diggs asked.

"That sun comes up, it's going to bring them renegades screaming down in our faces." He pointed toward where it would come up.

Diggs looked to the east, where the thin pink line had creased the horizon. "Sure enough?"

"I'm sure. Get plenty of ammo and then get under the

wagon. Celia, you get up in the box. It might turn back their arrows and weak loads in their guns—they didn't have repeaters yesterday.''

"I can fight with you. These are my cattle and horses."

He shook his head in disgust. She took orders worse than the men. *They* at least listened to him. What would Slocum do if he was there? Shorty wished he was there to help.

"I don't see nothing," Moore complained.

"They'll be here," Shorty said as he nodded to Adolph, who prepared to join them with his arsenal of handguns and the shotgun.

Shorty finally dropped to his knees and scooted in beside her under the wagon with some barrels and crates out in front for the crew's protection. The knot under his tongue was so swollen, it hurt to swallow. He unlimbered the Winchester, checking the round in the chamber, and then studied the golden crest of morning coming over the rise.

Their war cries shattered the morning. The yips of bloodthirsty wolves wouldn't have sounded worse. They swooped down like savage birds of prey, and the glint of the sun made it impossible to see. The glare was so bad it threatened to blind Shorty as he held his breath and waited for them to cross the last hundred yards. Goose flesh formed on his arms from the Indians' screaming.

"Hold your fire until they get in range," he said to his crew.

Then the rifles exploded, and the black-gray pungent gun smoke seared his eyes as rifles answered the screaming bucks. With the blazing sun in his eyes, he saw shapes of riders and horses to shoot at. There were cries of bullet-struck animals, and then only yipping as the surviving bucks rushed away.

"Anyone hurt?" Shorty asked, rising up on his knees to check on his crew. It had happened like lightning, and he felt shaken, unsure that that was all the Indians would do. They couldn't let their guard down—not yet.

"We're fine," Adolph said.

Shorty looked into Celia's pale face and nodded. "We did good that time."

"They coming back, you figure?" Thad asked.

Shorty nodded ruefully. "They ain't through."

"How many did we get?"

He rose on his toes and looked. "Three horses and two bucks lying out there. Boys, go careful—they could be playing possum on you—and see if they're alive."

"We will," Barley assured him.

"Don't take no chances. It can get you killed."

"We won't."

"What next, Boss Man?" she asked with her back pressed to the wagon and looking somewhat recovered.

"We've got a herd to move. Get something to eat and we better get to work."

"You've taken good lessons from someone," she said.

"I had lots of time to learn," he said, and then grinned. Damn, she was the prettiest thing he could ever recall. *Man, Slocum get back here and take over the reins of this outfit.*

"All dead," Diggs said, going by on his way to eat the food that Adolph had ready for them.

"Good. Two less to scalp us next time," Shorty said, and went to refill his coffee cup as the others came back.

"Did it spook the cattle?" she asked, coming to where he stood, leaning against the front wheel of the wagon and studying the country the Indians rode off into.

"No, I checked. They look like they're all there. It's a wonder they didn't stampede, but we could round them up if we had to. All of us here to do it."

"Will they come back?" she asked.

"The thing about an Injun, you don't think like he does. He might want to go home in the middle of a battle, and he does it. Then, by damn, he might not have a home anymore to go back to, and all he's got left to do is fight. Those are the real bad ones."

"Not any way to tell who the real bad ones are then?"

"Yeah, there is. You recognize them after a while."

"I hope they went home. Let's eat," she said.

"Fine." Engrossed in his thoughts of the cattle drive ahead of them, he blew on the coffee to cool it. "I hope they went home too, Celia. Hope they went straight home."

He looked up when Adolph brought him a plate. The aroma

reminded him he was hungry after all. It was sourdough biscuits in a sea of thick flour gravy with lots of browned meat floating in it. The man was a skilled cook, and not bad to have in a fight either.

"What's he do when he ain't cooking?" Shorty asked when Celia returned with her food.

"Farms. He raises corn and pigs."

"Terrible waste of such talent—" He blinked his eyes.

There were riders coming in. They wore hats and led a packhorse. Not Indians for sure, and he counted four of them. It was no trick—they weren't Indians, they were cowboys. He could tell by how they rode like loose sacks of potatoes in the saddle.

"Someone's coming!" Thad shouted.

"I see them," Shorty said. "I see them."

15

Light-headed, Slocum rode the bay. The melting snow made the sod boggy under his hooves. Meadowlarks flitted ahead of them, running off behind tufts of brown grass, giving their sharp whistles. A few prairie chickens had blasted the clear morning sky and drawn a smile from Feather as she rode the smaller roan close to his stirrup.

"You hear that?" he asked, turning his head to listen to what he thought were noisy ravens in the distance.

She nodded sharply. "Mules. Bad men come."

"Simon Bergereon?"

"You know him?" She frowned. Obviously, she didn't like the buffalo hunter and his men.

"Only met him once, and that wasn't under the best of circumstances. He wanted a corral I was using. We had some words."

"Bad man. He sells whiskey and cheats the Sioux."

"We better stay out of his way then."

She agreed, and they trotted their horses westward. The jar of the gait hurt his shoulder, but he gritted his teeth and rose in the stirrups. He had to get over this wound soon and find the outfit. Obviously there was no infection. She had done a good job tending the wound. He had to heal, and that was going slower than he'd planned. But worse yet, he worried they might be west of the cattle drive route, and heading in

97

that direction would only carry them further away from the herd.

He glanced over his shoulder. No sign of Bergereon and his outfit yet. They might make it away undiscovered. Slocum pressed the bay into a lope, and they soon gained the next crest. On the top of the rise, he reined in the bay and looked back. Nothing. Then, with a satisfied nod to her, they went on west.

Close to sundown, they found the remains of a dead horse and chased away the flock of ravens feasting on it To his relief, he also discovered tracks of the cattle. He felt much better when he dismounted and looked over the dead Indian ponies. Wolves and coyotes had hollowed out its intestines, but obviously it was an Indian horse with war paint and war signs on its hide.

"You know this horse?" he asked.

"It belonged to Crow Man."

"I'd say from all I can see that they must have attacked the cattle camp at this place."

"Your people's camp?"

"Yes, I recognize the weld in the chuck wagon rim track. They must have had a standoff here." He looked around and then shook his head. "No graves."

"They are foolish boys. They have been filled with many lies." She pursed her lips and made a distasteful face.

"What else do they have?" he asked.

She narrowed her eyes and shook her head. "Nothing but the reservation." She shrugged, and the buckskin fringe on her blouse gave a wave.

"Then warfare and death is the only thing left for them?"

"Yes. You have been there too?"

"Yes. I live that every day."

"Should we camp here?" she asked waiting for his answer.

"No," Slocum said, looking around at the last camp's remains. "We'd better keep movin'."

"Too late. They are coming," she said, and cast a glance over her shoulder to indicate the direction of their backtrail.

"I hear their horses," he agreed, considering what he had

to do next. What did Bergereon want? Maybe they were only
his scouts, out looking for whoever had made the iron tracks
in the soft ground.

There were four riders. He could see their outlines as they
drew closer in the last light of day. With care he checked the
loads in his Colt and reholstered it. Then he flexed his fingers.
That arm was sore, but he could use it—lots of things that a
man could do if he was hard pressed. What did Bergereon
want?

They drew up and sat their horses in a row, like vultures
on a tree limb at a Texas cow-butchering. Leering eyes as-
sessed Feather, and that made Slocum even more on edge.

"Aye, it's you, Slocum," Simon Bergereon said with a
sardonic grin. The rest of his men on horseback formed a
semicircle. The titter of their anxious laughter caused a cold
chill to run up Slocum's spine.

"What's your business here?" Slocum asked.

"Oh, we've got business, Slocum. Lots of business.
Where's your partner?" Bergereon looked around.

"Texas, I guess."

"You and Big Tits there are on a little trip, I see."

Slocum let the man's words shed off like so much rain, but
inside, a rising fire of anger knotted him up. "Whatever you
got in mind, Bergereon, get on with it. But I'll guarantee
you'll be the one that dies here."

"Brave words for a man way out numbered."

"Numbers don't count. It's who dies first. Were you in the
war?"

"Yes." Bergereon's dark eyes narrowed as he drew up the
reins to settle his horse.

"Then you've seen men die all kinds of ways. Only thing,
a bullet never found *you*."

"That's right. What're you getting at?"

"Death. Yours. She seen it three nights ago." He tossed
his head toward Feather. His plan to bluff the man had better
work.

"What the hell are you talking about?" With a dark frown
of black anger on his face, he forced his horse up until its
muzzle was in Slocum's face. "What's she know?"

"She's a witch and she rolled the bones. Asked me if I knew a big hairy-faced buffalo hunter rode a fat roan horse. I said, sure, that's Simon Bergereon. What's wrong?"

"What did she say?" he growled, but his voice had lost the sureness of before.

"Said he was going to die."

"When?"

Slocum was close enough to grasp the bridle rein in his left hand, then fill his other hand with his gun butt and shove his Colt into Bergereon's ribs. It all happened fast, and gave him a sharp pain in his shoulder that shut his right eye, but the tables were turned.

"Right now. Tell them boys to drop their weapons or you're dead."

"What are you going to do?"

"Kill you if you don't tell them to do it, right now! Ever see an army without a general? They go to pieces, Simon."

"Do as he says!" Bergereon ordered.

The horse tried to jerk free, but Slocum held onto the bridle. Then the shaggy roan twisted sideways and Slocum's back was exposed to the men.

The metallic click of a rifle being levered stopped Slocum's heart. Then he saw that Feather had jerked the Winchester out of Bergereon's scabbard and held it cocked and ready at her waist. The others dropped their handguns. Slocum jerked Bergereon out of the saddle. And then stood him up between him and the three men that she had covered.

"What do you plan to do?" Bergereon asked.

"Kill you if you try a thing. The rest of you get off those horses.

"Get their horses," Slocum said to Feather. "*You* get over with your boys." He gave the big man a shove to send him on his way. "Everyone back." With a wave of his gun barrel, they moved back in the fast-fading light.

She led their ponies over and looked at Slocum.

"Saddle our horses," he said. "We're going to leave these gents here to camp." He hated that too, for the night chill had begun to settle in with sunset, but there was nothing else to do but kill them or make tracks. He preferred to leave them afoot and ride after the herd.

"You can't leave us out here on foot!"

"Bergereon, I can leave you dead as easy as alive." He watched Feather run off in the twilight with the leather skirt flying to bring back their hobbled horses.

"I'll get you for this, Slocum, if it's the last thing I ever do."

"Shut up." A couple miles from there he would leave their horses, but they would be until daylight finding them. That would give him and Feather time to find the herd. If Bergereon was smart he wouldn't push it but the big man acted as if he would have to push it. In the end, Slocum's made-up lies about the bones might even come true. Time would tell.

She quickly had their animals saddled and their other horses in line. He stored the men's handguns in Bergereon's saddlebags.

"You can find these out there somewhere," he said, swinging up and nodded for her to take off.

Bergereon roared like a wounded bear after them. He'd get revenge. He'd do all sorts of things to him and her. Slocum ignored the man's ranting, and whipped the horses to make them keep up as he and Feather forded the small creek; they headed north in the growing darkness.

"I'm sorry," he said, drawing up beside her and checking one more time in the fading twilight for signs of Bergereon and his men. He couldn't see them. Good, he and Feather were going to escape.

"You should have killed them," she said.

Slocum nodded. She probably knew more then he did— cold-blooded murder wasn't his high card, even with worthless scum like Bergereon. He could always hope that someone else would do it.

Off across the starlit night, a wolf cried above the protest of their saddle leather and the drum of hooves on the soft earth. They'd have to ride far before they released and ground-tied the hiders' animals.

16

Warily, Shorty studied the tall lanky rider who dismounted from his horse. The other two looked younger and sat their cow ponies. Typical Texas drovers by their dress and saddles. Men a long ways from what they called home, and the hard looks on their faces had been sharpened, no doubt, by the past cold weather and snow.

"You must have been attacked by Indians," the man said, indicating the dead ponies and bucks.

"Yes." Shorty waited for the man to introduce himself. Something crawled in his guts about the threesome. He didn't know why, but he wished that Celia were back at the MC Ranch and Slocum was there to back his hand.

"Johnny Black is my name," he said, then removed his hat and said, "Howdy, ma'am," to her.

"Shorty Giles is mine. That's Miss McBroom."

"You the ramrod of this outfit?"

"Yes."

"Guess you're heading for Ft. Robinson with these beeves?"

"That's right."

"We're going there too. The boys and me. That's Mack and Joey. We're going there too, so if you don't mind we'll string along, help you drive these steers for our keep. Lots of Injun bands around, and I figure we'd be safer with you and

102

your bunch, plus you could use the extra guns and hands.''

Shorty considered the offer. With those howling bucks still out there somewhere, he'd be some kind of fool not to accept it. They were willing to ride along for their food—what could he lose having the extra guns? But if the newcomers were tied in with Diggs and Moore, he, Celia, and the boys could wake up with their throats cut. A risk he needed to be prepared to handle.

"Toss your bedrolls in the wagon," he said to the newcomers. "Diggs, you and Barley ride swing. Thad, take the horse herd. You gents need fresh horses, we'll cut you out some.''

"Mighty obliging of you, ain't it, boys?'' Black stuck out his hand and shook Shorty's.

It wasn't right. Something about the threesome had him bad upset, but he'd taken them on to help and he had to figure out how to outfox them later. Damn, he wondered where Slocum was as he scanned the hills. Nothing. There were no other options for him, with the Indians out there somewhere, but accept the new men and head the herd north.

"You figure them fellas doing this for charity?'' Adolph asked under his breath, bringing Shorty a last cup of coffee.

"No, they ain't. Keep your wits about you. Too damn convenient that they rode in like that. Unless they figured that they'd better protect the herd from them wild renegades.''

"Yeah, that's one way to look at it. I'll keep my shotgun handy.''

"Good. I'll warn Barley and Thad.''

"We should move better with that many riders,'' Adolph said, tossing out his dishwater.

"Yeah, you figure on about twelve to fifteen miles today before you set up camp. We need to get to Ft. Robinson as quick as we can.''

The new hands grabbed a few biscuits with meat off the tailgate and headed out to the herd on their fresh horses. Nothing on Diggs or Moore's part gave them away as knowing the new men, but Shorty planned to study them all closely.

"We've gotten lucky,'' Celia said, gathering up the iron posts with loops that made the rope pen.

"Don't like them." Shorty studied the new men as they rode out to take their places around the herd.

"Why?" She handed the pins to him to put in the box on the side of the chuck wagon.

"I think they're up to more than they are saying. Too damn convenient the way they rode in."

"How's that?"

"Call it a hunch, but I think they came in to save the herd from those renegades so they could steal it for themselves."

"Oh. What will we do?"

He closed down the lid and stuck a stick in the hasp. "You start riding close to me. Like a burr, understand?"

"You're serious?"

"Dead serious. I wish to hell Slocum was here and maybe he'd know what to do. Until then, you stay close and keep that peashooter handy."

"It's not a peashooter." She looked peeved over his remark, and slapped the small-caliber Colt in her waist holster.

"Fine then. It's too small to do much damage. Stay close to me."

"What do you plan to do?"

"They won't try anything until we get within a few days of Ft. Robinson. They need us to herd the cattle there as bad as we need them to help us."

"Then what?" she asked, mounting her horse.

"We have to turn the tables on them."

"How?"

"I'm working on that, gal, working hard." Shorty swung his chap-clad leg over the fresh dun. It bogged its head and for a half-dozen jumps made him pull hard on the reins. Then, with a deep groan, it settled down and loped in a tight circle. He brought it back with a sheepish smile for Celia.

"Didn't figure he had that left in him." They fell in side by side, and waved at Adolph as he headed around the herd with his mules and chuck wagon.

"You ever been married?" she asked.

"No."

"Ever been engaged?" she asked, an amused smile on her lips.

"No."

"You haven't done a whole lot with women in your life, have you, Shorty Giles?"

"Can't say as I have, ma'am."

"Did you ever want a place? I mean one of your own?"

The dun started acting up, and he set it down hard with the reins. "Quit that." Then he turned to her. "No, ma'am, I never thought much about settling down with a woman—I mean, a wife."

"Might not be so bad."

"What would a woman want with me?"

"You can't never tell." She rose in the stirrups and set her horse in a long trot.

Damn, he'd never talked to a woman like her before. She was talking serious things. He'd never considered the like before in his life. Oh, he'd been with plenty of sporting women in his time—but the likes of Celia McBroom was more than he could believe. What would her brother Bruce say to all this? He'd more than likely set her in her place the way he did with him and Slocum back at the ranch house.

Realizing she had left him, he booted the dun out to catch her, and it almost swallowed its head between its knees before he jerked it up. In a few yards he was beside her, and made the dun trot.

"A poor man come courting you, he might get hurt by that brother of yours," he said.

"I don't think you fear Bruce or anyone."

Shorty settled back in the saddle and considered her words. Damn, that girl could put one thing right after the other on his brain to fret over. No, he didn't fear much when it came right down to it—he avoided lots of trouble, but he never did turn tail and run away unless the odds were too lopsided.

His main worry for the moment lay with the Texas hands and what they planned to try. If they never got the chance to take the cattle herd—they might work for nothing too. That was the way he planned it. Them working for nothing suited him fine.

The day passed uneventfully. V's of honking geese passed overhead and Shorty envied them—no worries and headed south, where it would be warm. The clear azure sky, deep as any ocean, was without a cloud, and a warm south wind hurried the geese along.

"Making good time today," she said after rejoining him.

"We sure are. The extra help should move us closer every day."

"Still concerned?"

He bobbed his head. The day's share of worrying was about to eat a hole in his upset stomach. How would he handle the Texans? Adolph was a fighter, and those two boys weren't to be sniffed at. But the Texans were not Sunday school boys either.

"No solution yet?" she asked.

"Not yet, and no sign of them bucks either all day." He twisted in the saddle to look over their backtrail. "Maybe they decided we were too strong with these new hands."

"Maybe your assessment of those Texas cowboys was wrong?"

"I doubt it. It's like Slocum said when those first two came in. Them cowboys wasn't footsore enough to have walked as far as they said they did." He settled in the saddle and scowled at the horn in front of his lap.

"Diggs and Moore work every day."

"That's like these new ones. All some kind of acting."

Nothing she said would dismiss his mistrust of the new hands. Shorty still felt edgy about them. It was all too convenient for them to show up when they did, although their arrival might have saved the crew's scalps. The Indians hadn't been seen since the morning attack. *Damn Slocum, wherever you are, come on back.*

17

Slocum drew up the bay horse and studied the long line of cattle strung out across the prairie. The sound of their bawling had carried to him long before he and Feather topped the ridge.

"That is the herd?" she asked, drawing in the roan beside him.

"Yes, that's them." He looked over his shoulder, and in the bright midday sun saw nothing but the brown sea of grass. No sign of Bergereon. He nodded to her, and they set out in a long lope.

Shorty reined up at the sight of them and shouted to Celia, "He's alive, girl! Slocum's alive!"

The two of them came at a hard run. They met and slid their horses to a halt.

"This is Feather," Slocum said to introduce her. "This is Celia. That's Shorty."

"Where have you been?" Shorty asked.

"Shot. Feather saved my life, but I can tell you about that later. Who's the extra help?" He indicated the herd, having observed the extra hands.

"Some hands showed up yesterday after Indians attacked us. Johnny Black, Joey, and Mack. Why?"

"They may be the jaspers that shot me. It was snowing hard so I never got a look at them, but the bunch that shot me were the same ones that delivered Diggs and Moore close to our camp.''

"You all right?'' Celia asked.

"I'm healing.''

"You must be a good doctor,'' she said to the Indian woman.

"He is a strong man.''

"Yes, he is,'' Celia said, and acted satisfied. "What do we do next?''

"Play the hand out, I guess,'' Slocum said. "Any more trouble with the Indians?''

"No. They chased me back to camp yesterday when I went out to look for you, and then attacked again this morning. Did they pick up their dead?'' Shorty asked.

"I guess so. We found three dead ponies a couple of hours ago.''

"These new jaspers rode in then and offered to work for their keep to get to Ft. Robinson.''

"What in hell are three Texans going to do in the wintertime in Ft. Robinson?''

"I asked myself something like that. But help's help. I couldn't do anything.''

"You did fine, Shorty. They didn't get a good look at me, so they might not know I was the one slipped up on them. Besides, I remember hearing someone say they thought I was an Indian. Let's play it like Indians shot me.''

"Good enough.''

The women agreed with nods. Both of them talked to each other and ignored the men as they rode along. Slocum gave them a look, but turned away. They appeared busy enough.

"All of us need to watch them five from here on,'' Slocum said as the bay snorted wearily.

"Better cut out a fresh horse for you and her,'' Shorty said. "Them two look plumb tuckered.'' The two men set out in a lope for the horse herd.

"Mr. Slocum!'' Thad exclaimed as they rode up. "We all figured you dead.''

"Take more than a few Injuns to do that.'' Slocum watched Shorty rope a horse for him and lead it out. Then he dropped heavily from the saddle and began to undo the girth.

"Things been hopping around here too while you were gone," Thad said.

"I understand. New hands came in?"

"Yes, sir, but I can't figure what out-of-work cowboys are doing way out there."

"Good question. We need to keep an eye on them."

"I will. I still have that Colt you gave me. I keep it handy too."

Slocum's new horse was saddled, and Shorty waited with a fresh horse for Feather on a lead.

"That's her, ain't it?" Shorty said.

"Yes."

"I guess that horse trade you made coming up here worked out," he said as Slocum mounted up.

"More than you will ever know."

"She's a pretty woman. Seen that right off."

"Did I mention I had a run-in with Bergereon last night and left him and three of his henchmen on foot back about fifteen miles."

"No. The buffalo man?"

"Yeah, that's him." Slocum checked the chestnut. It felt good to have a fresh horse under him.

"What in hell is he up to?" Shorty asked.

"No good, I would say. Feather says he cheats the Sioux. Sells them whiskey, and we know about the rifles."

"Them bucks attacked us never had repeating rifles or we'd of been dead." Shorty made a scowl, and then he rubbed his upper lip on the side of his hand.

"They may have them next time. Thanks to Bergereon."

"I'll remember that too. I figure we've covered over half the distance to Ft. Robinson. That means in a week we should be there."

Slocum absorbed the information. That should give them at least two days before the Texans tried to take the herd. They needed to be within a few days of the fort for their small crew to drive the cattle in without trouble. He would like it much better if the women weren't in the way.

"Maybe we should send the women into the fort when we get, say, three days out?" Slocum offered.

"Not a bad idea." Shorty looked around to be certain the two women hadn't heard them. "I was worried about Celia ever since you left."

"Part of the job, amigo."

"Yeah, but I wasn't looking for no boss job when I signed on here."

"You did great, Shorty. Cattle are moving and we're halfway." Slocum glanced over at his friend with a grin to cheer him up. Somehow the look on Shorty's face did not convey that he was satisfied.

With the herd in hand, Slocum decided to go on ahead, and he and Feather rode on to find Adolph and the night camp. In twenty-four hours he had had less than a few hours sleep. His sore shoulder ached, but they skirted the herd and made good time. They found the German set up on a small freshlet, busy cooking, and he grabbed his shotgun off the drop table at their approach.

"Slocum, am I seeing you?" He blinked in disbelief, and then he set the scattergun back. "Can't be too sure out here."

"I understand," Slocum said, and dropped heavily from the saddle. "This is Feather, and we haven't had much to stuff in our bellies in the past few days."

"Come on, I'll fry some bacon. I have some cold biscuits?"

"That will be fine."

Adolph wiped the large cast-iron skillet out with his apron tail and set it on the grill. "Won't take long. Some potatoes too?"

"We'd appreciate it. Feather saved my life."

"Glad to meet you," Adolph said, and then busied himself cooking for them.

Slocum squatted down beside the man. "What do you think about the new hands?"

"Don't know much," Adolph said, and laid the snowy strips of fresh-cut bacon in the bottom of the skillet. "But they don't look like men out on the line looking for work."

"How is that?"

"They only took half the cold biscuits and bacon I set on the tailgate for them this morning."

"You saying they ate something before they got here?"

"Yeah. I seen cowboys ride in before off the grub line. They eat everything you put out and some of the wood off the wagon."

Solocum nodded thoughtfully. Less than a week left in the drive and he had plenty to find out about the new hands.

The food filled them. Feather nodded her approval between bites. Adolph hovered over them, his large pot of sumbitch stew boiling in the giant kettle.

"Got to cook plenty for this big a crew."

Slocum agreed with a nod, his mouth full.

"You want to try some stew? It is about ready."

"Sure, we'll eat a small bowl." Slocum shared a look with her. She approved.

"Been a long time since you ate?" Adolph said, and then he laughed.

"Too long."

"You mentioned your shoulder. Do I need to look at it?"

"You can. She did wonders for me. Got the bullet out with a ramrod had a screw on the end to extract bullets out of a barrel."

"Bet that felt good." Adolph made a pain-filled face.

"It worked."

Adolph and Feather rewashed Slocum's shoulder and the wound area. Then Adolph applied boric acid, along with some petroleum jelly, and rebandaged it.

"It isn't infected and is healing," Adolph announced.

"I've got two doctors now." Slocum shook his head as he rebuttoned his shirt. Neither of them heard him. Adolph was busy talking to her about the boric acid. She was busy talking to the man about willow-bark tea.

Slocum removed his bedroll from his horse and spread it out on the groundcloth. He planned to get a few hours sleep before the herd arrived.

"Wake me up when the crew gets here," he said.

Both of them whirled around and looked at him as if they didn't know he even existed. He shrugged them off. He was too weary to say anything else. In the blankets, he shut his leaden eyelids and slept.

The cattle bawling awoke him. Sharp smoke from the campfire made his eyes tear. Feather had taken another roll to sleep on sometime after he'd lain down; she sat up sleepy-eyed too.

"They're coming in," he said, and threw back the covers. Still groggy and stiff from his nap, he flexed his sore right arm; the discomfort was not as bad.

"Will we stay with them?" she asked, pulling on her moccasins.

"Yes, until the cattle are to Ft. Robinson."

"Where will you go then?"

"I have no home. Do you?" he asked softly.

She shook her head. "But I know of a place in the mountains. The cabin is warm if no one has burned it down."

"Far from here?"

She nodded as if the distance was too far.

"Perhaps when the cattle are at the agency . . ."

"We will see," she said. "I must make you some willow tea."

"I am fine."

"I see the pain in your eyes when you move your arms. Don't lie to me." In a bound, she was on her feet and headed for the campfire.

"Are you a witch?" he said after her, but she never bothered to reply.

The afternoon had warmed up to summerlike temperatures. He leaned his butt on the wagon wheel and drank her sharp-tasting concoction. Idly, he studied her shapely butt under the leather as she bent over the tub and washed dishes for Adolph. There was a fine form in those buckskins. Maybe a winter with her in some lodge in the mountains would beat sunny San Antonio.

"Slocum!" Barley shouted. "I figured they had killed you." The youth dismounted and rushed over. "Good to see you."

"You boys been doing fine without me."

"We been doing. Whew, now we have all this help, we

can sure make it. Why, Shorty said you've had Indians after you too."

Slocum told his story as if the Indians had shot him. He met the new hands as they came in and the men gathered around to drink the fresh pot of coffee.

"I want to thank all of you," Slocum said. "We're well on the way to Ft. Robinson, and I guess that with this many men we can have three night-riding shifts a night and all of us get some more sleep."

"That's good news," Thad said, and the others nodded.

Slocum did not recognize any of the new hands from the snowy encounter. They didn't show any concern or undue curiosity at his return. He would have known the man who spoke at the fire, but none of them sounded like him. Were they mere cowboys riding the grub line, or were they rustlers? Only time would tell.

"Do we need to bring in the horses?" Celia asked.

"I ain't seen a sign of those renegades all day," Shorty said. "Any of you boys seen them?"

The head shakes around the semicircle answered him.

"I'd rather be safe than sorry," Slocum finally admitted. "I think we better drive them in at dark and corral them. They scatter our remuda and we'd be in deep trouble for horseflesh."

"Guess you're right," Shorty agreed.

"Better eat now!" Adolph announced. "Come and get it."

"Thought you'd never say that," Diggs said with his tin plate in his hand ready, first in line.

"I am glad that you're back," Celia said, standing beside Slocum.

"Thanks. Kind of nice to be here."

She shook her head ruefully. "We have made this drive before, and never had a problem besides half burying the chuck wagon in a river crossing."

"We may still do that."

"I thought that time was bad." She drew a deep breath. "Things can be worse, can't they?"

"I hope we have the bad times behind us."

"So do I, Slocum. So do I."

He looked across the prairie to where the late afternoon sun hung in the sky. The longhorns were all scattered out and grazing. They had a few hours left before dark—maybe the worst was behind them. He only hoped that included the Sioux renegades and Bergereon.

18

The next two days of the cattle drive passed uneventfully for Slocum. Weather warmed to summerlike temperatures as they moved northwestward. He studied the Texans like a hawk as they worked around camp, and never detected anything suspicious. They simply acted like normal cowboys—grunted, groaned, complained, and laughed. Still not satisfied they weren't part of the rustlers' plot, he went on overseeing the operation. There was no sign of the renegades or Bergereon either—a fact that did not disturb him, but he kept them in the back of his mind. In the middle of the afternoon of the second day, he joined Shorty at some distance behind the two women riding drag. He'd noticed that a bond had developed between Celia and Feather. At times their laughter and chatter reminded him of girls in their teens and drew a smile to his cracked lips.

"I figure that we're about forty to fifty miles from Ft. Robinson," Slocum offered as he rode beside his friend. "There's those hills ahead like Adolph promised us this morning."

"I been seeing them. What's the plan?"

"Tomorrow I want to send the two women ahead to the fort. Then, if anything happens, they won't be in the way."

Shorty narrowed his eyes in distrust. "Strong-headed as they both of them are, you think they will listen to you?"

"If these new hands are the rustlers, then the two women

need to be at Ft. Robinson. The Texans can't deliver her cattle for sale there if either of the women are already there.''

"Won't be worth stealing them, would it?" Shorty smiled at his discovery, and agreed that the plan suited him.

"That's the whole idea," Slocum said.

"It might work. Convincing the women to go up there and then fooling the rustlers. Good plan, wish I'd thought of it myself." Shorty took off his wide-brim hat and scratched his thin hair.

"You would have in time," Slocum said to reassure him.

Shorty reined his horse back and shook his head. "I used up all my thinking power ramrodding this outfit those days you were gone."

"You did good."

"I got by is all. Slocum, you tell me the God's truth—you figure a fella like me would have a chance courting her?" He indicated Celia, who was a hundred yards ahead chousing poky cattle.

"A man can't tell," Slocum said. "But if you've got the notion, go do it."

"I may. I just may do that." Shorty looked off toward the herd lined out ahead as if in deep thought on the matter.

Slocum considered the situation as they rode along. Celia might be ready for a man of her own. Obviously her relationship with Bruce was more one-sided than she wanted to admit aloud. One thing for certain. Shorty had to be smitten to ever ask such a personal question, and it must have been eating him up besides. Slocum drew a deep breath of the prairie's grassy smell. There was something new on the wind besides the odor of cattle and horse. He was smelling cedar or pine from the hills before them. They should find Adolph and the chuck wagon over the next rise—he was ready for it.

The sight of the distant chuck wagon's white top in the sun and wisps of camp smoke cheered Slocum up. All day the wound had knifed him with discomfort, much more than usual. He flexed his stiff back in the saddle, and then he pushed forward to help the women make the slackers hurry and catch up.

Some cattle in the rear were slow walkers; others were footsore or had been foundered. Then a few obvious ones wanted to hang back, not go with the herd. They would try to break off and graze, anything but be part of the herd. Those steers tried the patience of the drag riders. Swinging his rope, Slocum drove in a spooky one who had cut away to eat.

"I would kill him," Feather said about the steer, which had a particular slashed black marking on yellow brindle hide.

"He's always breaking away," Celia added.

"Adolph needs some beef, we may do that," Slocum said. "Tomorrow I want the two of you to ride into Ft. Robinson and make arrangements for the herd's arrival."

They looked at each other, then at him, with frowns.

"You don't want us here if they try to take the herd," Celia said after looking around to be certain they were alone.

"No. If you two are there, they can't take the herd and sell it to the government. Wouldn't do them any good to steal it."

"Smart idea. We may go to Ft. Robinson. Where are you going now?" Celia asked.

"To look around and be sure we aren't being followed. Keep that business about you two going to Ft. Robinson a secret. I don't want them double-guessing me." He turned in the saddle. "Shorty, you handle drag for a while."

"We can do that," Celia said, and shared a nod with Shorty.

Slocum considered the notion for a moment. "Feather, come on. Your eyes are better than mine."

He set out, heading for the rise a mile away. He glanced back as Feather came on his horse's heels, a broad smile on her face. He could see Shorty busy talking to Celia as they rode behind the herd. Good enough.

On the hilltop, he dismounted and used the brass telescope from his saddlebag to look over their backtrail. Nothing showed in the lens. There was no sign of Bergereon or the renegades, but the fact that they weren't visible still made him uneasy.

"Where did the war party go?" he asked her as he collapsed the scope and returned it to his saddlebag.

"Perhaps to the reservation ahead." She dismissed his question with a shrug.

"To get more help?" The sun forced him to turn his head to look up at her.

She shook her head. "Maybe they want to do something else."

"Maybe. Three days and we'll be at the fort with these cattle. Tomorrow I'm going to scout those hills ahead. I don't want to ride into a trap."

"I will go with you." she said sitting her horse.

"No. It would be better if you go to Ft. Robinson with Celia and learn all you can about things there."

"About Bergereon too?"

"Yes. I suspect he has plans that could endanger lots of lives in this country."

She slipped lithely from her horse and looked about the empty land. Then, in an instant, she was in his arms. She removed his hat and pushed the hair back from his forehead.

"I would go with you when the cattle drive is over," she said. "You know that?"

He nodded. With her ripe body pressed to him, he considered the time ahead. What would he do afterwards? Go back to Texas and winter in San Antonio? Or should he accept her offer?

"This place you speak of?" he asked.

"Maybe four days ride." She threw her fringed arm to the west. "Maybe more."

"Big Horns?"

"Yes," she said breathlessly, and cupped his face in her long palms. "We could spend much time in your blankets."

"Come spring—"

Her long fingers on his lips silenced his protest. "Then I would have your son inside me." A glint of excitement danced in her eyes.

"I could never stay to raise him."

"I would raise him. He would know both worlds and you will be proud." She pressed her forehead into his vest.

Try as he might to clear his brain, the truth would not leave; she was serious. Shaken by the knowledge of her sincerity, he held her tight. She wanted his son. He was a man with nothing but a past, no home, and damn poor prospects of a future. No roots, nor could he plant any. Some well-worn wanted posters from Ft. Scott, Kansas, carried his name, and two determined bounty hounds hounded his backtrail; the Abbott brothers, Lyle and Fred, were somewhere out there at that very minute. Like bloodhounds, they never gave up. The pockets of the man whose son had died were lined with gold, and he kept the Abbott brothers' expenses paid.

"You know—sometime—I'd have to move on?" he finally asked her.

She raised her brown eyes to look at him. "Yes, but I want this."

"Damnit, girl!"

She looked behind his back with her hand over her brow to shade her eyes, and searched in the direction of the herd.

"Good, they are gone," she said at last, and in long strides ran to his horse. Her nimble fingers began to untie the leather strings that held his blanket-slicker roll. She paused and glanced over her shoulder at him for his approval, and he nodded.

His breath came quick as he considered what she intended to use the blankets for out here in the warm sunshine. The swirl of her long fringe like windswept willow, the inviting curves of her body, the thoughts of her firm flesh in the grasp of his hand, all caused his excitement to increase.

"They are all out of sight." She waited with the roll clutched in her arms.

"Here?" he asked in a small voice, shaken by the notion, but already committed to a downhill course toward the inevitable. Who gave a damn what they did out here anyway?

"Who will tell them? The horses?" she asked, fluttering the blanket into the wind. Then she bent over and spread it on the ground. That task completed, she stepped into the center of it.

A grin spread over his face, and he nodded to her in mild approval. "Perhaps the red-tail hawk out there will tell on us?"

"No, he is a friend of mine."

"Good, we need friends."

She looked at him. The corners of her mouth twitched with a smile. Then, with devilment dancing in her eyes, she bent over and slipped the fringed dress off over her head. She pulled off the leather garment on her arms, then gave a toss of her thick braids back over her molded shoulders. Her firm, long brown breasts shook in the sunlight for his inspection as she slid the dress off. With their gazes locked on each other, she dropped to the blanket and removed her moccasins. Then, one leg at time, she stripped off her leggings. Her head held back, she braced herself with her arms behind her. The sunlight gleamed on sleek skin.

He fumbled with his shirt buttons, then toed off his boots. In his stocking feet, he unbuckled his gunbelt and let it slide to the ground. His movements to undress were purely mechanical, for his eyes and total fascination were centered on her luscious body.

He dropped to his knees and faced her as she hugged her knees and looked at him—hard.

No time for words. His breath raged in and out of his lungs like a man starved for air. His hips ached to pound her with all of their force, and his stomach churned with the excitement.

Slowly her legs melted away, and as a well rope draws a bucket, he pulled her into his arms. He drew her up until her rock-hard nipples bored holes in his chest. Until her mouth was inches from his, and then he plunged his face to hers and sought her lips with unbridled desire and hunger.

The prairie was gone, the world, the cattle, the hawk, the screaming killdeer, everything but two people's raw needs bent on satisfaction. All the rest swirled by them. Her muscular tongue clashed with his, and the heat of her passion transferred into a consuming rage.

His right hand cupped, molded, and reshaped her breast. He sought the nipple and tasted it. Her fingers combed his hair, and then cradled his head as she savored his attention. They both trembled with pent-up desire. His mouth traced down her centerline, and she reposed back on the blanket. With her eyes closed in dedicated devotion, she moaned as his mouth sought her belly. At last, he spread her legs apart and found her flower.

She screamed when he kissed her there; she half rose and then, with both hands, tightly clutched his head to her. In a deep entrancement, she lay back in submission, her legs wide apart. He reared up. With his breath ragged and his strength impaired, he looked down at the dark mound of hair and the pulsating slit that glistened in the sunshine

It was time for action. He moved forward on his knees. With his root encased in his fist, he began to ease it into her swollen gates, his hips aching to lunge like a bolt of lightning deep inside her. But he held back, making slow, easy intrusions into her well-lubricated passage until he passed her ring. When the nose of his manhood parted the tight circle, she gave a sharp moan; then her hips rose to meet him, and she cried out even louder.

"Oh, yes," she gasped; then her mumbled words were in Sioux. But he could tell they were encouraging him to go faster, even harder, and were only the outpourings of a woman intoxicated with passion.

They made love like giant, spiraling dust devils. Like the whirlwinds that tore up the ground in their spinning vortex, they sought the same thing from each other's body. His butt was driving his spear deeper and deeper into her target. Her muscular belly was high off the blankets, her back arched toward him as she sought him, grinding their pubic bones together. Time and again she cried out, then lapsed into a strained faint, and after a while recovered for a new flight, and again, like a moth caught in a flame, withered into a pile under him.

At last all their fires were exhausted. They lay spent on the blanket. His hand affectionately squeezed the right cheek of her hard butt.

"We need to find that place you speak of when this cattle drive is over," he said, and then he closed his eyes.

19

"Hey, took you two long enough," Celia said, riding out to meet them. "Feather and I are going to ride upstream and find a private place to bathe."

"Sure. Be careful. We might have missed something out there," Slocum said.

"We will," Celia said, and turned to Feather. "Let's ride."

Slocum watched the two women race across the prairie to the east. Side by side, their horses thundered away. He was wrenched away from the sight by Shorty, who rode up beside him.

"Didn't see anything out there?" Shorty asked.

Slocum shook his head. "Come daylight, I intend to search those hills ahead of us."

"Figure they might try to ambush us?"

"Those bucks that attacked you earlier haven't got a buffalo to eat out here. Have you seen one since we left Ogallala?"

"Seen a few stray bulls the first day. Come to think of it, none since then." They rode into camp and dismounted.

"If you were Indian and not on a reservation, what would you do?"

"Change my diet to beef, I guess."

"Exactly why I'm riding out in the morning."

Shorty lowered his voice after checking around. "Then if

these fellas are the rustlers''—he gave a nod toward the men busy catching fresh horses for their night herding—''then they ain't got an outfit out there to come help them?''

''Not that I could see this afternoon.''

''So that means if they've got a gang out there, they've got to be over a day behind us too. It would be hard for them to catch up, huh?''

''Right.''

''Then''—Shorty took his hat off and spun it with the end of his finger up inside the crown—''all I've got to do is keep an eye on them five rannies.''

''Right. And any renegades that I miss.''

Shorty slapped his hat back on and jerked down the brim in front. ''I can handle things on the drive then. You've got to be damn sure there ain't no arrows waiting for us up in them hills.''

''I will.'' Slocum leaned over. ''Keep my leaving a secret until sunup so they can't make any plans too fast.''

''Oh, yes.''

''How far is the next stop tomorrow?'' he asked Adolph aloud as he and Shorty prepared to try his coffee.

''We go fifteen miles. Wide valley up there, plenty of water, and usually got grass there too.'' Adolph indicated the hills, busy turning a Dutch oven with a potholder and a J-hook. ''Good place to camp there.''

''Two more days driving get us to the fort?'' Slocum asked, coming over to the campfire.

''No, it takes three.'' Adolph shook his head, raised up, and mopped his sweaty face on the apron tail as he stepped back from the fire. ''Whew, it's hot. Last place to stay is an old homesteader's place called Tucker's. He ain't there no more. Bruce usually held the cattle there until time to sell them. The Injun and cavalry horses eat all the grass off at the fort.''

''That makes sense.'' Slocum turned to Shorty, who agreed.

''Where are the women?'' Adolph asked with a frown.

''Went upstream to bathe,'' Shorty said, bending over for the coffeepot with his kerchief in his hand.

"I better ride up that way and see about them." Slocum headed for his horse. "No sense taking any chances."

"I better come along too," Shorty said on his heels.

"No." Slocum turned and shook his head. He needed Shorty there with the cattle. "You watch the herd and them hands. Anything's out of order, I'll be back and tell you."

He swung up on his horse and headed east. How far would the women ride? Chances were good they were having fun splashing in the chilly creek. The sun was back up to summertime temperatures, and a good dip in the small stream wouldn't be so bad. But not with either of the females along. He chuckled to himself as he loped the big chestnut. The boys called the big horse Doc. Cowboys hung monikers on everything. They called some old steer that acted like a bull half the time His Lordship, and another black and white one that bossed the others around they'd christened Napoleon. Doc was a good solid gelding, a better ranch horse than most, and as trail boss Slocum could take his pick.

Where were those women at? He rose in the stirrups and scanned the country ahead of him. The gully that fed the small stream grew deeper, and he could see from the tracks that the women had ridden into the foothills. He crossed the creek several times, keeping an eye on the tan walls that towered above him, clad in gnarled cedars with some spindly pines.

He leaned over and read the two horse tracks. They'd be around the next bend, he felt certain. Coming around the corner, he spotted clothes hanging on a tree limb and reined up.

"Hey! We were worried about you!"

He waited for their reply. But there was only the rush of the small stream over the rocks, and he scowled. With his hands cupped around his mouth, he repeated his warning. No answer.

"All right, girls, here I come, dressed or not!"

Doc splashed his way up the creek. His shoes clacked on rocks under the surface. Slocum ducked, passing under the limb that held Celia's skirt and blouse. Feather's buckskin clothing was draped on a box-elder bush. The water hole was empty.

"Hey, I'm here," he shouted, standing in the stirrups and looking around.

Above him, some ravens called, and it echoed in the canyon. He peered around, certain that the women planned to surprise him or something. Where were their horses? He booted Doc up on the bank, and looked at the small flat under the thin pines for any sign of them. Something caught his eye in the dirt between some of the rock outcropping—horse tracks.

In a flash he dismounted, dropped to his knee, and examined the ground. Three unshod horses' prints were in the soft earth. Fresh sign. Either the damn renegades had the women, or Bergereon did. He couldn't think of a worse result either way. Feather could handle the renegades, but Bergereon . . . it would be bad either way. In a bound, he was in the saddle. He paused to gather their clothing, then remounted with Feather's buckskins over his arm, and caught Celia's things off the tree from the saddle.

He would need help if it was the buffalo hunters who had the women. Could he afford to leave part of the crew at the herd while they chased the hunters down? His arms loaded with clothing, he ducked and dodged as the pines tore at him in his headlong flight down the canyon. No time for turns and twists. He needed to get back and gather help. No telling what they would do to an Indian squaw. He didn't want to think about it, and booted the chestnut on down the craggy way out of the canyon.

"What is it?" Shorty shouted as he ran out to meet him.

"Bergereon has kidnapped both women," Slocum said, looking for Adolph as the rest of the crew came on the run.

"I need a sack, Thad, for their clothes," he shouted to the boy.

"They took them naked?" Johnny Black asked in disbelief, taking the clothing from him.

"Unless they had other clothes. Shorty, you stay here with the herd. Thad, Johnny, Diggs, and Moore ride with me, we're going after them. The rest of you, stay here with Shorty and help hold the herd. I don't figure you can move them with so few riders. Barley, come first light in the morning, you ride for the fort and tell the commander what's happened. He can send a company of men down here and help you get the cattle up there.''

"What if you don't find them?" Shorty asked, looking bewildered.

"We're staying after them until we do. You boys coming with me get a Winchester from Adolph—we're going to need it when we catch up with them. A box of ammo apiece too,'' Slocum said. "Get your bedrolls out of the wagon, men, this may take sometime.''

"I got the rifles here, boys.'' The cook's arms were full of Winchesters, and he began dispensing them. The men were rushing about helping each other, getting horses, rolls tied on, and ready to leave.

"You think you and that boy will be all right with them rannies?'' Shorty asked under his breath.

"We better be, or someone won't come back alive.''

Shorty nodded that he had heard him. "I guess that's right. Hope you find them two before anyone is harmed.''

"I'll do what I can.''

"Know you will. I'll take care of the steers. Don't worry about them. Damn, I wish I could do something.'' He dropped his voice. "Good luck, Slocum.''

Slocum nodded. He needed bodies, men behind rifle butts, when they confronted that buffalo scum Bergereon. That was what he needed the most; the rest he could handle. Finding the women was his first order of business.

The kidnappers didn't have a great head start. An hour at the longest—lucky he'd gone to check on the women. It could be a trap too. That crossed his mind as they prepared to leave. Bergereon was no fool. He had plans, and they didn't include Slocum's welfare. He narrowed his eyes and considered the sun in the west. Less than two hours left of daylight. They needed to hurry.

20

Slocum led the way. The riders filed behind him. Deep shadows had invaded the canyon, and he watched the towering walls with suspicion. It was a great place for an ambush, but the only way in, and judging from their tracks the kidnappers had been moving along at a trot anyway. He'd spotted the tracks of the women's shod horses too. They only made the anger rise inside his chest. If they hurt one tiny finger of those women—he'd never rest until they were all dead.

"How far you reckon they'll go tonight?" Johnny asked behind him. He was a tall lanky Texan, and Slocum suspected he was the only one smart enough to be the ringleader of the rustlers. Still, neither his voice nor that of any of the other newcomers reminded him of the night of the shooting. Maybe he was mistaken.

"A ways," Slocum said. "I figure that Bergereon knows this country and we don't."

"You figure we'll find him?"

"We'll find him unless he takes wings."

"Wouldn't be a bad idea to have some."

Slocum agreed. He hoped they wouldn't be this exposed when the trail came out on top. The skin on the back of his neck itched; they were damn sure vulnerable on this narrow path on the side of the mountain. It would make a perfect ambush site.

He breathed easier when they topped out and rested their hard-breathing horses. Somewhere in the distance some ravens cried. He turned his ear to the wind that whispered in the pine needles. No sounds or signs of the hiders besides their hoofprints. They'd halted in a thin stand of open pine, and a turpentine smell saturated the air. He leaned over in the saddle and studied the tracks that went east on the ridge-back.

"I figure there's a half dozen of them and the women," Black said, walking along, studying the tracks and leading his horse.

"That's my notion too." Slocum shifted the holster on his hip and looked over at the dismounted men busy relieving their bladders. He decided to join them, and stepped down.

"How tough are these fellas?" Diggs asked, busy rebuttoning his pants and then hitching up his chaps.

"Plenty tough. They're buffalo-hiders."

"How are we going to take them?"

"I guess however we can. We've got to find them first." Slocum finished peeing and replaced his buttons.

"Yeah, and it'll be dark soon. No moon till after midnight either."

"We'll go a ways and then see. I'm not for riding off any mountain in the dark."

"Me neither, but anyone would hurt them women ain't worth much, are they?" Diggs asked.

"No, not worth a buffalo turd," Slocum said, and mounted up.

Darkness settled. They had ridden several miles and were still on top of the range. Slocum halted them and dismounted heavily. He had hoped to find the kidnappers by this time. Obviously Bergereon had a place chosen and aimed to ride there. Slocum undid the latigos. He was filled with dread. He didn't want to think about the two women without their clothing in the grubby hands of those horny hiders.

There was nothing more he could do until the moon rose. That wouldn't happen for four hours. If they rode on, they chanced falling off the side of one of these hills and plunging to their death.

"Thad and I want to scout ahead," Black said.

"Be careful, and don't let them see or hear you if you get close," Slocum answered, deeply engrossed in his concern for the women's safety. "Oh, Thad, you armed?"

"Yes, sir."

"Good. You two find something, you come back here and get us."

"We will," Black said, and the pair went off through the silhouettes of the pines.

"We build a fire?" Diggs asked.

"No, they might see it. Wrap up in your blankets. Thank God it isn't as cold as it was before."

Slocum dug out a cigar from his saddlebags. He licked the length of the tobacco cylinder, and then torched it with a shielded lucifer so the flare would not be obvious. A man looking hard in the night could spot a lucifer's light at a great distance, a fact that had saved Slocum's life before.

Hayes, Kansas, was where the ambusher had become bored and struck a lucifer to light his roll-your-own. The brilliant orange flare had lighted the entire alleyway. When he saw the match, Slocum had eased back into the shadows and slipped between two buildings to the street, taken a horse at the hitch rack, and ridden away. Thirty feet further and he'd have been in the man's gun sights.

He drew on the stoogie, and the rich sweet smoke filled his mouth. The other men gnawed on the cold jerky and biscuits that Adolph had sent with them. Black and the boy had gone off eastward, and Slocum hoped they found something, but he felt certain the kidnappers were still miles away. With a slow small space in his lips, he blew out a stream of smoke. The nicotine relaxed him and he was grateful. His mind filled with a jumble of ideas, while his guts were upset and on edge over the women's safety.

"When the moon comes up, we ride," he told the men in a quiet voice since sound carried a long way in mountains like these.

"Better get some sleep then," Diggs said.

"Worse than driving cattle," Moore groaned. "On the go, on the go."

Slocum didn't bother to answer him. Maybe he had mis-judged Black. Maybe those men were just riding the grub line looking for work. He'd have to see. He would never forget that voice he'd heard the night those rustlers shot him. Diggs and Moore had to have come from there. The rustlers spoke of Diggs and Moore having to work the cattle. What was it someone said? *They'll get their share.*

He drew on the cigar until the tip of it turned rosy red, and then he inhaled. Slowly he let the smoke escape his lungs. He had to ease off. Even rustlers wouldn't put up with men kidnapping women.

He had taken a seat with his back to a pine tree when he heard footsteps coming. Were the two returning? He rose and drew his Colt.

"Who is it?" he called softly.

"Us, Slocum," the out-of-breath Thad said. "We found their camp."

"The women all right?"

"No," Black said between gasps. "We better get down there fast."

"How far away?"

"A couple miles. We ran most of the way," Thad said. "Too many for us to handle, but they're drinking a lot and that might be good."

"It's that bad?" Slocum asked Black.

"Yes, sir."

"Come on, boys, bring them Winchesters," he called to the others. "We got some cleaning up to do."

Slocum followed on Black's heels. The men hurried across the mountaintop. He had to stop and let Thad and Black catch their breath.

"It was bad," Thad said. "We had to stand—stand there." He broke into a deep cough.

Slocum waited for the boy to recover.

"They were hurting them—" Thad managed, and shook his head.

"Come on," Slocum said to the others. "Black, you and Thad come on at your own speed."

"No, I want to help you catch them," Black insisted. "They're just a mile or so over this rise."

"Then we better keep our voices down."

"Yes, sir."

Slocum heard the kidnappers a long time before he saw them. There were drunken shouts, and when he peered into the canyon, he could see the roaring fire with sparks and flames licking into the night air. Black and the boy had done well. But his thoughts quickly turned sour. There, on the blanket, he could see a snow-white ass humping away on top of someone. They had both women staked out on their backs and were taking turns raping them.

He raised the rifle and considered putting a bullet in the man's butt.

"You can't shoot, you might hit one of them," Thad said in his ear.

Slocum agreed with a nod, and let the rifle down. What good would it do killing one of those studs and hurting one of the women? He considered a plan. But it took so damn long. His bunch would be a half hour getting downhill and in position around the camp to take the kidnappers. Still, for the women's welfare, that was what they had to do.

"Black, you and Thad go down that side. Diggs, you and Moore come with me. Be sure we don't shoot each other or the women."

"Makes me sick," Diggs said. "Why, they ain't no better than damn dogs."

"I agree, but we've got to be careful."

Their heads nodded that they understood his plan. Then Celia's scream of horror shattered the night, and they separated. Moving in a crouch, the men headed through the thin forest to reach the camp below. Slocum tried to swallow, but the knot behind his tongue was too thick. His foot slipped, and he wondered if the small avalanche of gravel off the hillside would warn the kidnappers.

For a long moment he stopped and listened. But their raucous shouting and howling continued. With a nod to the other two with him, he went ahead down the hill. They reached the bottom, and moved to the side behind the horses, which were picketed between two trees. Slocum decided they could approach the camp from behind the tent, keeping it between them and the fire. Anyone that broke and ran, they could keep from getting to the horses.

He wished he had given a signal to Black so he'd know when Black and Thad were ready. Slocum held up his hand for Moore and Diggs to wait. Give Black and Thad a few more minutes to ready.

The sounds of the revelers was loud.

"It's my turn on that gawdamn squaw!" someone shouted.

It will be your turn to die. Slocum's fingers closed on the trigger guard. Then he rushed around the front of the tent.

"Hands in the air!"

"Why you sumbitch—" A whisked hider reached for the Colt at his waist. Three rifles fired at the same time, and the man made a shocked face and then wilted to the ground. The roar and blinding cloud of gun smoke filled the moonlit clearing. Someone fired a pistol, and the lead whizzed past Slocum's ear. He saw the man for an instant and shot, but knew before he squeezed the round off that the man was rolling away.

A tearing sound behind him made him whirl.

"They're getting out the back of the tent!" Diggs shouted, and the roar of rifles shattered the night. Horses screamed and the blinding residue of the black powder burned Slocum's eyes. He set the empty rifle down and started around the tent with his Colt in his fist.

"Get the hell out of the way!" someone shouted.

Slocum ran head-on into the chest of a bolting horse. With nowhere to go, the animal struck him and sent him sprawling on the ground. Before he could gain his feet, a second horse and rider flew past him. He quickly rose to his knees and took him. Two-handed he emptied his .44 after the rider into the night. But it all was to no avail. Two of them had escaped, and were probably unscathed.

Filled with anger, he ran across the camp reloading. He punched out cartridges and refilled from his belt. He slid to his knees as Thad used a large jackknife to cut the bonds on Celia's hands. Diggs brought a blanket and covered her.

"Slocum, is that you?" she asked in a rasping voice.

He took her in his arms. "It's me. You'll be fine."

"No, I'll never, ever, ever be fine again," she sobbed, and hugged him.

"How is Feather?" he asked with Celia in his arms.

"She's conscious," Black said. He wrapped her in a blanket as he and Diggs helped her up.

Slocum looked around. "Did they all get away?"

"No," Moore said, holding a rifle ready. "I got one here and one is out cold."

"Two of them's dead or going to be," Black said, helping Feather over to where Slocum was holding Celia.

Feather's blank eyes settled on Slocum's and she nodded. "I want to kill them," she said in a dry, hoarse whisper. Then she tucked the blanket in around her and sat close to him.

Slocum looked down at Celia as she shook in his arms. He wet his lips. Then he handed the white woman to Feather so she could comfort her.

"You hold her." He pushed to his feet as Black dragged a hider over by the collar. "Bergereon and Randolph get away?" Slocum asked.

The quaking skinner never answered.

"I said, did Bergereon and Randolph get away?"

"Slocum, don't let that squaw have me. Shoot me, but by Gawd don't let her have me." The man trembled and clasped his hands together. "Sweet Jesus, man, don't—"

With a fistful of leather, Slocum pulled the man to within inches of his face. "You low-life bastard, talk to me! I asked you did Bergereon and Randolph get away!"

"Yeah, they rode out—"

"You screw them women?" He drew the man up on his toes.

"Yeah, I did."

"Good, because that will be the last thing you ever do on this man's earth." He gave the man a shove, and the hider landed on his knees begging and pleading with him. "Don't let the squaw have me."

"I say we hang all four of them," Black said.

"Two of them's dead," Thad said.

"Be a waste of a rope," Moore said, still holding the rifle on the hider.

"I'd buy the damn rope," Black said.

Slocum looked at the two huddled women. Their misfortune knifed him deep in the chest.

"Someone take one of their horses that wasn't been shot and ride back to our camp," Slocum said. "These women need their clothing. May as well bring all our horses down here too."

"I'd like to go get them. I ain't never hung no one before," Thad said warily.

"I'll go too," Diggs said, looking pale in the firelight.

"I'll help string them up," Black said.

"Don't make me no never-mind," Moore said.

"You two go get the horses," Slocum said, and chunked some more wood on the fire.

"This other one's coming around," Moore said, and stirred the groaning hider with his boot toe. "Get up, you lowlife."

"I'll get a horse to hang them on," Black said, and went by Slocum.

"May not be any left," Slocum said.

He went over and squatted beside the dazed man on the ground. "What's your name?"

"It's Delf," the other prisoner said quickly.

"What's *yours?*" Slocum frowned at the man.

"Darby, Woodrow Darby."

"Well, Woodrow Darby, help Mr. Delf up."

"You ain't letting that squaw have us?"

"Get him up. I'll ask the questions."

Shaking and jerking, he aided Delf to his feet.

"You rape either of those women?" Slocum asked Delf.

He shook his head warily and looked away. Still unsteady, he clung to Darby and tried to draw up, but at last slumped his head down without speaking.

Slocum stepped in close, drew his Colt, and stuck the muzzle in the man's face. He cocked back the hammer, and the man looked cross-eyed down the barrel. His whole body began to shake.

"Yeah. I screwed one," he said.

"Good, I'd hate to hang an innocent man. Tie their hands behind their back, Moore."

"I'll do it."

Slocum turned and walked away. He was breathing rapidly. Then he realized the cocked revolver was still in his grasp. Bergereon and Randolph wouldn't get far. They would pay the price.

With care, he lowered the hammer, spun the cylinder until the empty would ride under the hammer, then replaced the Colt in his holster. He went back to the blanket where the two women huddled, and he knelt down.

"What can I do?" he asked.

Feather, holding Celia in her arms, rocking her like a baby, just shook her head. "It is not your fault," she answered in a low voice.

He said nothing, and rose.

"You two made your peace with your maker?" he asked the hiders, seeing that Black had two ropes over the pine limb at the edge of the fire's great flare.

"I'd like a drink of whiskey," Darby said, acting relieved that Slocum wasn't letting Feather have him and wetting his lips.

"Get moving. You can get that in Hell," Slocum said.

Delf half stumbled, still acting groggy, but Moore steadied him and half dragged him to the tree. Black had fashioned nooses on the ropes. One at a time, Slocum and Moore put them on the men's necks, situated the wraps at their left ears, drew them tight, and then hoisted the men up on the horses while Black held the animals heads.

"You bust one, I'll bust the others," Moore said, and Slocum agreed.

With a loud "hee-yah!" from Moore and Slocum, both horses bolted away in the night and the hiders danced their last set on the creaking ropes. Slocum didn't bother to watch.

21

"She going to be all right?" Shorty asked with a concerned frown after they made Celia a pallet in the chuck wagon.

Slocum nodded. "It'll take time. But we all heal."

"I never knowed such rotten devils."

"You say Bergereon and Randolph escaped?" Captain Rynning asked. The straight-backed military man and his company had joined the operation just as Slocum and the other men returned with both women.

"Yes, they managed to get to the horses and ran through us."

"She going to sit out there all day?" Shorty asked with a toss of his head.

Slocum turned and looked back at Feather, wrapped in a scarlet blanket and seated on the rise below the camp. "I guess so." It would take some time for both women to recover; he had no idea how deep the scars of their being violated ran, but he knew without asking them that they were hurt deep. Hanging their attackers had not brought them any solace; they barely acknowledged the fact. He wondered as he considered the matter if turning the two hiders over to the Indian woman would have let her vent a portion of her inner feelings. He wished he knew.

"I am sending a messenger to the fort before nightfall to report this incident and have those men arrested," Rynning said. "Perhaps a company of soldiers can intercept them."

"Be a good idea," Slocum agreed. "I guess we have enough hands now, Captain, to drive these cattle into the fort."

"We'll ride along then and help. The prospect of fresh beef has my mouth watering."

"Adolph says we need to stop at at a homestead this side of there and let them graze there until the receiving agent wants them."

"Tucker's, that's a good place. We came through there. Plenty of grass and water."

"That will be our plan." Slocum turned to Shorty, who quickly agreed.

"Very good, see you later," the captain said, and went to join his men.

"I ain't figured one thing," Shorty said, lowering his voice. "Do you still think Black and them rannies were going to try to take the herd?"

"It was too damn convenient, them all showing up. They may have had their plans changed with the army coming and the rest."

"I just wondered."

Slocum shook his head. "If I ever hear that voice again, I won't forget it."

"I'd bet not. You want some coffee?"

"Believe I'll take my cup up on the hill and sit with her a while." Slocum nodded toward Feather.

"I may see if she needs anything." Shorty motioned towards the wagon and Celia.

"Good idea."

Slocum walked slowly carrying two cups of coffee, one with three scoups of sugar in it for Feather. It was too sweet for him, but he knew she liked hers that way. He stood above her, and at last she looked up with her dull eyes.

"Sweet coffee," he said.

She reached up and accepted it. Then he dropped to the ground and blew on his own coffee to cool it. The wind had risen, and there was chill to replace the once-warm sun setting in the west.

"We'll be there soon?" he asked.

"Yes."

"Can we go to this place in the mountains?" he asked.

"You don't have to humor me."

"I'm not."

"I wish I could wash what they did away."

"It is like the leaves in fall. Let the wind take them."

"Slocum, you can say that, but for me it is different. Even for Celia it is different." She dropped her head and shook it as if there was no escaping her worst feelings.

"Maybe the spirits in the mountains would take it away. This bad spirit inside you."

"I wanted to go for you." She raised her chin, but did not look at him.

"Then we shall go there."

She raised up, scooted on her knees, and then threw herself at him. He caught her in his arms, spilling his coffee; he dropped the cup and drew her up to hug her. She buried her face in his vest and began to cry. It was the first time since she had been rescued that the tears flowed from her eyes and her strong body racked in great tremors as she sobbed aloud.

This was deeper than a small hurt. It had been locked deep inside, and had escaped only in the security of him holding her. His arms tenderly cradled her and kept her close. He wished he had words to heal her torment and make her whole again.

"You want to go with me after what you saw them do?" she asked, wiping away the wetness on the sides of her hand as he fought to undo his neckerchief for her.

"Damnit, Feather, I said I did." At last he managed to strip the silk cloth free of his neck, and tried to blot the tears coursing her brown cheeks.

"You mean it?"

"Yes, I don't care about what happened. I wanted to punish them and I did four of them. They gave their lives for that. Either the army or I will get Bergereon and Randolph, and they will pay too. Nothing more I can do."

"This place is far away."

"I have all the time."

"When you leave me—"

He frowned at her.

"When the geese come back," she explained.

"Oh, in the spring." He understood her meaning: when things began to thaw.

"Don't tell me, simply go." She threw her arms around him and pressed her face and torso hard against him.

"I will do that. I will do it that way," he said, and laid his face on top of her head. The wind sent strains of her long hair whipping in his face. *I will do that, Feather.*

22

"Ten cents a pound," Shorty repeated. Then he spat in the dust. Why, the damn cheap sumbitch was cheating her out of at least two cents a pound on every head. He looked around for Slocum as Celia continued to talk to the officer in charge of purchasing.

"Lieutenant." Shorty finally managed to get his raging temper under enough control enough to speak to the man in a civil tone. "These are fat cattle. Not some south Texas culls been eating mesquite and prickly pear."

"The Army Quartermaster's Corps is only paying ten cents per pound on the hoof, sir."

"Don't make any sense at all. You haven't got enough beef to sop up a biscuit left around here and we have the only cattle. The honest-to-gawd fair price for them critters up there is twelve cents plus a pound, and I think you are taking advantage of the—"

"It will be all right," Celia said, and took him by the arm.

"No, it ain't—" But Shorty felt himself being dragged away by her.

At some distance she turned and looked back, Shorty's arm still locked in hers, and called sharply to the lieutenant. "We will have the first cattle here to weigh in the morning."

"Yes, ma'am. I will have my men assembled to receive them."

"I need the money to pay the mortgage," she hissed at Shorty.

"Two cents more would help that a lot."

"That lieutenant is not going to pay two cents more, and perhaps not even buy my cattle at all, Shorty, if you keep on. I can't risk that." Lines formed in her smooth forehead as she tried to impress him with her concerns.

"Celia, I only want what is best for you. And twelve cents is dirt cheap. Ten cents ain't even wages for fattening them."

"I'm sorry, Shorty, but the army isn't going to pay any more and they also buy the beef for the Indian agency."

"I'd bet my pay that the lieutenant's charging the army more than ten cents." The anger still had not subsided inside Shorty; he felt riled, and only some sort of revenge would suit him.

"That's accusing him of stealing," she said. "Don't upset him. I need the money from this sale."

"Listen, they need that beef too. They won't get any more until spring, and then it will be stringy as all get-out. They need to pay you a fair price for your top beef." He looked around the small business district for a sign of Slocum. Nothing. Where had he gone? Slocum would know how to deal with these officials. Damn, where was he when Shorty needed him?

Up until that lieutenant had offered her ten cents a pound for those cattle, Shorty was sure feeling that he and Celia were going to be really close after this drive was over. He'd only lost his temper because he was so concerned for her, but he'd fight wildcats over being cheated by some damn boy who wasn't green behind the ears.

"We will bring the first quarter of the cattle in tomorrow," she said, and patted his arm.

"Yes, ma'am," he said, unenthused.

"Shorty, you don't understand. I have a mortgage to pay on the ranch in Ogallala that is due next month. I can't— where are you going?"

"Inside the telegraph office for a minute."

"Whatever for?"

"I'm going to wire Ft. Lincoln and ask the quartermaster there what he'll pay for beef."

"What will that prove? We're miles from there."

"You just bear with me."

"I don't understand."

He went in with Celia behind him and walked up to the operator, a fresh-faced lad barely out of his teens who stood up behind the counter.

"Young man, I want to sent a wire to Ft. Lincoln to the quartermaster."

The young man smiled at Celia, and then pushed the pad and lead pencil toward Shorty. "We can do that in a few minutes. The wire is open right now, sir."

"Good." Shorty disengaged his arm from hers and took the pencil, licked the lead, and began to write.

QUARTERMASTER FORT LINCOLN STOP HAVE 500 PRIME BEEF ON THE TRAIL STOP WHAT IS DAY'S QUOTED PRICE PER POUND ARMY WILL PAY FOR DELIVERY TO YOUR HEADQUARTERS QUESTION MARK SIGNED S GILES MC RANCH FORT ROBINSON NEBRASKA

"I should have an answer in a few hours," the operator said after reading it out loud.

"That's good. I will check back later. Thanks."

"Sir, sir, that will be thirty-five cents."

"Oh, yes," Shorty said, feeling a little red-faced that he had not thought of paying the man for the service. "I'll be back early in the morning to get the reply."

Outside on the boardwalk, his arm in tow, Celia jerked him to a stop. "You lied. You said they were on the trail."

"Celia, honey, I just didn't say what trail."

"I still don't know what it will prove."

"If he answers and gives us a price, it's going to prove whether that shavetail is lying to us or not about the rate per pound they will pay."

"So what will you do if he is?"

"Depends."

"On what?" she asked, loosening the reins of her horse from the hitch rack.

"If the quartermaster at Ft. Lincoln is higher-ranking than this boy, I'll rub his nose in it." He boosted her into the saddle and went for his own horse feeling much better. Sometimes things had a way of working out.

"And if not?" Celia asked, turning the horse. "What then?"

"We eat crow and take ten cents."

"I doubt you've gained a thing." She shook her head in disapproval.

Shorty whistled out his breath. "It only cost thirty-five cents to know, didn't it?" He twisted around. Where had Slocum gone? They had ridden to town with him and Feather. Shorty and Celia set out in a long trot. They needed to get back to the herd.

"Ten cents?" Slocum frowned at the price. "Highway robbery, but you did great. I'd have never thought to wire Ft. Lincoln." The two men and the women were holding a parley back at the cow camp.

"Shorty's been trouble all day," Celia said in disapproval. "I thought he was going to beat that poor lieutenant up."

"Now Celia." Shorty shook his head with concern. "I was only looking out for you."

"What did you and Feather learn up on the agency?" Celia asked Slocum while hugging Shorty's shoulder affectionately to show her concern.

"They think that Bergereon is headed for the Powder River country with his guns, and then will run to Canada after he sells them to hostiles."

"The army going to cut him off?"

"They have patrols out. But he can avoid patrols like an Indian," Slocum said.

"So he's going to get away scot-free?" Shorty dropped his head, shaking it ruefully. "Damn, that's a rotten shame."

"He hasn't got away yet. I understand that Lieutenant Judson Schaeffer is coming with a special troop of cavalry. I think that Bergereon's gunrunning has upset the army enough. They are going to try and stop him.''

"You learned all that at the agency today?" Celia asked with a frown.

Slocum nodded. "We also learned that those bucks that attacked you all have gone west to join Sitting Bull."

"Good riddance," Shorty said. "Where's he at?"

"Powder River country, I guess."

"We have to out out a hundred steers tomorrow, drive them up to the fort, and weigh them," Shorty said.

"Let's hope your telegram works." Slocum smiled. He glanced over at Feather, who was seated on the ground wrapped in the blanket despite the afternoon sun's warmth. She remained in her shell, but time would heal her. That was all he could hope for.

Before dawn, the cowboys were saddling by starlight. Dutch ovens clanged, and Adolph rushed about stirring, frying, and baking breakfast. It would be a long day for the crew. Shorty was to take the first consignment to the fort.

"Water them good in that last creek," Slocum said. "At ten cents a pound, water's cheap."

"I figured on that." Shorty busied himself buckling on his bull-hide chaps. "What are you going to do all day?"

"Keep an eye on things around camp."

"You ever figure that rustling deal out?" Shorty asked under his breath, hitching the chaps around his waist.

"No, but when Celia gets paid, I'd have a plan for keeping the money safe."

"I hadn't thought of that."

"Be easier to steal the money than it was the cattle."

"Damn, you're right." Shorty raised his eyebrows and sighed. "Takes two heads to outthink them, don't it?"

"Helps when they work at it." Slocum clapped him on the shoulder. "You and the lady are getting along, I see."

"Yes, that's the good part. I kinda dread her brother finding out."

"Finding out what?" Slocum looked around to be certain they were alone for the moment.

"I figure if she'll marry me, we'll get hitched up here and he can lump it."

"Good idea."

"Never thought I'd be a Nebraska rancher, but there is plenty of grass up here, and I guess you get use to cold like you do the heat in Texas."

"Tolerate it, Shorty. Tolerate it."

"I could tolerate lots of things for a life with her."

"I believe you can. Good luck today."

"Boss Man?" someone called out.

"I'm coming," Shorty answered, and they parted.

At mid-morning, Shorty reached the telegraph office and dismounted. The cattle were coming. He could hear their bawling on his backtrail.

"I'll only be a minute," he said to Celia, and went inside.

"Got your answer," the operator said, and jumped up to hand him the paper.

S GILES MC RANCH FORT ROBINSON NEBRASKA STOP COULD USE TWICE THAT MANY FAT CATTLE STOP PAYING 15 CENTS WITH ONE CENT PREMIUM ON CATTLE CARRYING GOOD FLESH STOP WHEN CAN I EXPECT DELIVERY QUESTION MARK QUARTERMASTER IN CHARGE FORT LINCOLN DAKOTA TERRITORY CAPTAIN A. C. FURITIER

"Any reply?" asked the operator.

"Yes." Shorty dug in his pocket for fifty cents. "Send him one saying thanks but I will deliver them here, and sign my name."

"That will only be one quarter," the operator said.

"Keep the change," Shorty said, and rushed outside.

"What did you learn?" she asked anxiously.

"I learned the price of beef is higher in Dakota and so is the rank."

"What now?"

"Celia, let me handle the lieutenant this morning."

She grasped the saddlehorn and looked at the ground. For

a long moment he wondered if she was going to rip the horn out of the fork, her gloved hands were clasped so tight. Then she raised her face and made a small nod.

"That's being called dutiful?" she asked.

Shorty grinned and patted her leg before he mounted up. "I don't reckon you'll ever be *dutiful,* but I can't say that's what I want either."

"Mr. Giles, proceed."

"Yes, ma'am." He squinted off toward the fort and the area where they would hold the cattle. "I been thinking. You ever think hard about what I mentioned the other night?"

"Getting married, you mean?" she asked in a low voice.

"Yes." He didn't dare look at her. If she denied him outright, it might be more than he could stand. Maybe she would simply postpone doing any deciding.

"There are things you need to know," she said in a low voice.

"I don't give a damn about wash-water that's been throwed out." He wet his cracked lower lips. Would she or wouldn't she?

"That wouldn't bother you later?"

"Only things bothering me now—"

"We better get up there and see that officer." She booted her horse by him.

His heart stopped. No way she was going to accept his offer. He'd be headed back for to Texas in a few days, and Celia McBroom would be a dream that had evaporated like a dust devil that went over the hill. Damn her.

She turned a few yards ahead of him, reined her pony up, and then looked back at him. "I'll marry you, Shorty Giles, here or wherever you want."

"You will?"

He let out a war hoop. Then he charged his horse up to her, reached over, and took her in his arms and kissed her. His actions almost unseated the both of them. When he drew back, he saw the red on her face, and sheepishly looked around at the crowd that had rushed outside the businesses to see what was happening. On the sidewalks there were swampers and barkeeps, two Chinese men, three dance hall girls, a couple of buffalo hunters, a Jewish peddler, and six dirty-faced kids all staring at them.

"We're getting married!" Shorty shouted, and swung his hat over his head. His rebel yells were joined by rifle and pistol shots from the onlookers. His horse went to pitching, and almost unseated him. No matter. Nothing would dampen his spirits. It was the best sober drunk he'd ever experienced.

23

Slocum spotted the company of soldiers coming. The yellow guidon flag and the orderly rows could not be mistaken in the sunshine. Cavalry horses and soldiers made an unmistakable sound; well-oiled leather creaked and armaments made a certain clack with the horses' stride that Slocum would never forget.

"Company, halt!" the large red-faced sergeant ordered, and Schaeffer gave him orders to let the men water their mounts in the creek. With a salute for his noncom, Schaeffer dismounted and walked over, pulling off his gauntlet gloves.

"So you're cattle driving."

"I sure am for the moment. Nice to see you, Lieutenant. I heard you were coming."

"So much for secrets in the military." He took the cup of coffee Adolph handed him. "Thank you."

"Didn't learn it from the military," Slocum said. "Learned it up at the agency from the Indians."

Schaeffer shook his head, and then he noticed Feather seated nearby. "Guess you have an inside track up there?"

"Sioux. She knows the people."

"Did they say where Bergereon is at?"

"No, but he has four less men with him. Him and some of his men kidnapped her and a white woman, Celia McBroom, three days ago. Harmed them. I won't go into details.

We caught them in camp. Randolph and Bergereon got away from us, but they didn't have the pack train with them, so it must have been moving toward the Powder River country west of the Black Hills.''

"You're sure that's the direction?"

"Same ones told me that as said you were coming." Slocum smiled. "They said he was going to meet Sitting Bull and his bunch out there, sell him the repeaters, and then Bergereon would go to Canada."

"He could get lost up there."

"Either place."

"Thirty men is not much against the Sioux nation or even that bunch with Sitting Bull." Schaeffer dropped his chin and sighed out loud.

"I kind of figured your only chance is to head Bergeron off west of the Black Hills," Slocum said.

"Want to ride with us?"

"Can't. Where are your scouts?"

"I am supposed to get new ones up here."

"Good luck."

"I'll need every bit of it. Thanks for the coffee," Schaeffer said to Adolph, who was busy at the chuck wagon. "See you, Slocum."

"Ride easy," Slocum said, and the officer departed for his men at the creek. Slocum watched the troopers ride out, and wondered how Shorty had made out on his first day's weighing.

Thad rode in. He and Moore had been left behind to keep the cattle contained. He watered himself at the wagon barrel, then led his horse over.

"Everything going smooth?" Slocum asked.

"Yeah, I've been listening to the talk from those Texans."

"Learn anything?"

"A man named Roost or Rust or something is supposed to meet them in Ft. Robinson."

"What does that mean?"

"They said he would be there is all I heard."

"Thanks for the information," Slocum said. "Be careful."

"Oh, I will. They never let a thing slip before. I heard

them saying that when they were saddling up. That he would be there. Meet them." Thad started to remount.

"I figured there was one more of them anyway," Slocum said. "I've never heard that voice since they shot me, but I'll know it."

"Hope you find him."

"I will." He watched the boy short-lope back to the herd. He now knew that his hunch wasn't wrong. They had planned to rustle the herd after all. Next thing would be to steal the proceeds—he better look up this Roost or Rust fellow.

"I am going to town, want to ride along?" he asked Feather.

She nodded, still locked up inside herself, and rose to join him.

"Adolph, watch things," he said, holding her horse for her to mount.

"I will." Adolph waved them on.

At midday, they reached the small town that served the fort. The cattle weighing was under way. He could hear the sounds of cattle bawling in the distance. He dismounted at the saloon and sent Feather with some money to the mercantile across the street. "Stay over there in the shade on the porch until I come out," he said.

She nodded and stuck the money in her pocket. Without a word, she crossed the dusty street and disappeared into the store. Damn, he wished she would come out of her shell—it would take time. He looked at the green bat-wing doors. The red-lettered sign over his head said, DEVIL'S HOLE SALOON. COME IN AND CATCH HELL!

He parted the doors and looked over the empty tables and chairs. It was cooler inside the interior. He walked to the bar and ordered a rye. He was about to ask the bartender about the man he was looking for when a man in a black frock coat came out of the back room.

"Bring me a bottle of good whiskey and a glass," he told the barkeep, and the familiar tone of his rough voice made Slocum drum his fingernails on the bar. His man was there. He turned with his elbows on the bar and studied the man. He had never seen him before that he could recall.

"You bring those cattle up?" the man asked, pouring himself a drink.

"I'm part of that outfit."

"Cattle I saw go by this morning looked fat."

"They had good flesh considering the weather we've had."

"Roster's my name. You the head man?"

"Just helping. Shorty Giles heads it up."

"How many hands?"

"Seven or eight."

"I heard they belong to a woman. You like working for a woman?"

"Work's work," Slocum said, turning back to his drink.

"I guess so. She'll be laying you all off, I guess, next few days?"

"I imagine that's so. We only hired on for the drive. You have any work?" Slocum glanced back at the man for his answer.

"Me?" Roster asked. He shook his head.

Slocum downed his drink. The last man in the deal had arrived. Three days and the cattle would all be sold. The money would be paid to Celia and then things could get serious. Roster obviously was the boss of the rustlers. Damn, he would have sworn Black and the others were straight when they took on Bergereon and his bunch, but then the hiders' actions were enough to rile up even outlaws.

He walked outside, and saw Feather across the street talking with several Indian women from the agency on the front porch. The blanket was on her shoulders, not over her head, and she looked more at ease than at any time since the incident in the canyon. He glanced back at the bat-wing doors. Roster had his plans. There were no riders up and down the street save for a few Indians coming in to trade. Slocum led their horses over to where she stood talking.

She broke off her conversation and joined him.

"You could visit," he said. "I am not in any rush."

"No, we were through."

"Had lots to say," he said, handing her the reins to her horse.

"Women talk. They mentioned the sack of gold that he would pay for the new rifles."

"Sitting Bull?"

"Yes."

"Where did he get gold?"

"Stole it from the men who stole it from the Black Hills," she said, shrugging off his question.

"I understand. Let's go back."

"Was he in there?" She reined up the horse and her dark eyes darted to the saloon.

"Yes."

She nodded, then threw the blanket over her head again and looked forward.

"Do you need to kill him?" she asked.

"I am not judge and jury. He shot me because he thought I was sneaking up on him and probably an Indian on the scout."

"What does he plan?"

"To rob her, I suspect."

"Do those others work for him?"

"I suspect so. Let's get back to camp."

Slocum looked off toward the northwest. The crowns of the dark Black Hills lay that direction. He could see their outline. Some tops were even touched in snow. Bergereon was up there somewhere. Sitting Bull's gold would coax him out.

Three more days should complete the weighing. Shorty would tell him when he came back to camp. Slocum dropped heavily from the saddle, and Feather began to undo her latigos. Inactivity ate him up. Wondering what Roster would do, wondering how the weighing went—it all bored him close to disgust.

He took a nap under some spindly pine, and was awakened by the sound of a galloping horse.

"Slocum, come quick," Barley said, jumping off his lathered horse. "Shorty needs you. Johnny Black's been shot and the boys had them a big fight at the Devil's Hole Saloon in town."

"What happened?"

"Black got into it with this fella at the bar."

"Was he wearing a black frock coat?"

"You know him?"

Slocum nodded. What in the hell was happening? Had the outlaws gotten into their own war? It didn't make good sense. But nothing had made much sense since they'd arrived in Nebraska with the horses.

Feather was already saddling his horse for him.

24

Shorty and the boys were gathered at the small graveyard on the edge of town. Slocum looked the somber crew over before he dismounted. He took a quick tally of the crowd. The older hand Mack and the kid Joey were there. Moore was missing, but Shorty and Celia were waiting.

"What happened to Moore?" Slocum asked under his breath as Shorty intercepted him.

"He rode out with this Roster guy who shot Johnny in the saloon."

"They get into it?"

"Yes, Joey said it was over robbing Celia of her cattle money. Johnny said he wasn't having any part of it, according to what I heard. Celia and I were across the street in the mercantile, and when I rushed out this Roster and Moore were riding off."

"Cream comes to the top," Slocum said. "More ain't no loss. Them other two, they sided with Black?"

"They said so, and told me Diggs was riding for her too, and wanted no part of the robbing business."

"Now we know who our friends are anyway. How did the weighing go?"

"After I showed the lieutenant my telegram from Ft. Lincoln, I got her fifteen cents a pound across the board."

"Good, your plan worked out good. We better get Black

planted and get back to camp. Those other two might try something else.''

"Right."

Slocum read some psalms over the grave. Then they covered the body up. Johnny Black was planted in the hard Nebraska ground without a headstone. Slocum thought about that for a long while. Black had been a cowboy, a drover, had helped recover the two women from Bergereon, had sent a few men straight to hell, and had redeemed himself in his last hours from anything wrong he'd ever been involved in. Had had loyalty. Had worked for the brand. The rocks clanged on their shovels as they covered him up and Shorty planted the cross made from carton lumber.

It read, ''Johnny Black—good man.''

Slocum went back to the horses and Feather. They mounted up and turned their horses toward the cow camp, standing in the stirrups and trotting their animals. They would split out more cattle in the morning. The job would be half over. He recalled Roster again. That man would bear watching out for. Slocum recalled his voice. He would never forget it.

The next day, the next shipment of cattle was cut out, and only Barley remained in camp with Slocum to watch the herd scattered up and down the valley. They needed Diggs to help them drive the cattle in and separate them at the pens. Shorty promised no one was going to wet their whistle in that saloon until the cattle sales were completed.

Celia rode along with him. Slocum almost laughed to himself over the change in her. Why, that girl had turned halfway into a tame wife already. He chuckled to himself, savoring Adolph's coffee and knowing this would be the next-to-last day they'd be there. The old homesteader's cabin with low log walls and the sod roof needed some repair. The corrals were fallen in, but the grass was strong in these hills and in places along the creek where a man could fence, irrigate easily, and sow alfalfa down the bottoms. A man needed a source of feed come deep winter this far north. Folks were just beginning to understand this north country. A man would need to make hay to ever survive up here.

''What are you thinking?'' Feather asked, and took hold

of his arm. Then she laid her forehead on his shoulder.

"How sweet alfalfa smells when you mow it," he said.

"I have smelled the small purple flowers and the crushed leaves too."

"That's what this land here needs." He indicated the valley around them.

"When will you plant it?" she teased, unable to suppress her smile.

"Oh, when I get time."

"No. You have to stay and keep the elk and deer away. You must cut and stack it too. I have seen such work."

"Other white men will come do that."

She hugged him. "You will ride on again, won't you?"

He nodded. *I have wanted to stay, Feather. It ain't been that at all.*

At midday, he and Feather rode hard around the perimeter, sending some steers back that had gone away from camp. Slocum was satisfied they were simply drifters and just needed tending.

He reined up, and she came off the hill after him. With a smile on her face, she swung the blanket from her shoulders and wadded it up in front of her.

"That is enough herding?" she asked.

"Yeah, that's the only ones I saw out of place. What?" He blinked at her as she looked around.

"Time to use this blanket," she said, and then smiled at him.

"I wondered what the hell you been carrying it for," he said aloud, and dismounted, tying his pony to a cedar bough.

"For you, of course," she said, and unfurled it on the grass that grew in the small glen.

"Good thing," he teased, and began to toe off his boots. "I was going to find another squaw."

She shook her head. "A short fat old one?"

"Yes." He reached out, took her by the waist, drew her to him, and kissed her hard. "A short fat one like you."

She tried to break free from his arms, but he held her and laughed. Soon they were on the blankets, kissing and savoring the warm sun in each other's arms.

He knew this was her test. But he wondered what she expected from him. He wanted her satisfied that the past was over with him and over for her and that the new day would dawn and they would be as before. How to do it eluded him.

"Slocum?" She brushed the long strands of hair back from her face and looked him in the eye. "We are going to the mountains?"

"Yes, and we will watch the snow sift down."

She pulled him down on top of her and raised her hungry mouth to his. Their world went blank and their bodies meshed. In the end they lay on their backs exhausted, spent, and groggy.

"When can we go?" she asked, reaching for his hand and then squeezing it.

"Soon. Very soon."

The next day passed slower. Slocum shot a fat mule deer for Adolph, and Feather helped him skin and dress it. She rolled the skin up after carefully fleshing it.

"A few more will make a shirt for you," she said. Then both of them turned and watched Celia riding hard up the valley.

What was wrong this time?

Celia reined up and gasped out of breath, "The Abbott brothers are at Ft. Robinson and looking for you."

"Who are they?" Feather asked.

"Bounty hunters from Kansas," Slocum said.

"Shorty sent you money and said for you to hightail it. Those are his words."

"I don't need Shorty's money."

"I want to pay you for all you did for me," Celia said, pained. "I'll pay you what I owe you, Slocum. He was upset—Shorty, I mean. Told me to ride out here because they wouldn't suspect a woman warning you."

"Shorty worries a lot."

"Here, take this. It is a hundred dollars. I must owe you more."

"Celia, you don't—"

"Take it, damnit, and cut out some good horses. Two apiece so you two have reserves."

"Shorty tell you that too?" he asked her softly.

"Why, of course. That man doesn't think I have a mind left."

"You two getting married?" Slocum hesitated as Feather raced for their horses.

"Yes."

"I wish I could give you away."

"That's sweet. Bruce won't like it, but I don't care."

"It ain't for him to like or dislike. You and Shorty have a good life together. When I come drifting through, I may want a meal or two."

"Anytime, come by anytime, Slocum."

"You and him be careful. That Roster and Moore are waiting for the money."

"We will," she promised. "You and Feather do the same."

"We're going to," he said as Adolph came over with a new Winchester and two boxes of cartridges.

"You may need these."

"Been my pleasure, Adolph."

"You come by Ogallala, you can stop by and eat my food."

"I'll do that," Slocum promised, and shook the man's hand.

With an extra horse apiece on a lead, Slocum and Feather headed for the Black Hills. The Abbotts wouldn't find their trail for days. Slocum looked back as the attractive Celia waved to them. Shorty would be a lucky guy; lots of woman under that split-tail riding skirt. Slocum urged his horse on, and laughed at the wind in his and Feather's face. Good-bye, Nebraska and the hills. They were Dakota bound.

They made a camp late that evening, and the next sundown, after a hard ride through the badlands, they entered the Black Hills. Inside the mountains of her gods, they camped on a pristine small stream that teemed with small silver trout. Feather noodled them out with her hand. Then she fried them and they ate several for supper.

•   •   •

Shorty stood with his hands folded over his chest and solemnly watched the shavetail quartermaster lieutenant count out the money to Celia. He shifted his weight from one boot heel to another. Almost eighty thousand dollars. He didn't know that much money existed in the entire world. Fifteen cents a pound times an eight-hundred-pound steer times all the cattle in the herd made it a rich business. Why, she probably hadn't paid over fifteen dollars apiece for them two years before when they were trailed up to Ogallala from Texas. And that sale to her had made that drover richer than the devil because he'd only given the Mexican brush-poppers who brought them out of the mesquite and spiny thickets two dollars apiece.

She placed the money in the canvas money belts until both were bulging. Then she handed them to Shorty, who nodded to the lieutenant, and they left the office.

"It's a small fortune," she whispered, keeping a bridle on her enthusiasm.

"How much do you owe?" he asked, looking both ways as they hurried to their horses.

"Less then fifteen thousand on the ranch and everything. Oh, Shorty. We are rich."

"What we going to do with this money?" He felt the weight of the money as a large threat to their safety even riding back to camp.

She looked around. "Hide it somewhere. I cut some old newspapers the size of the money. We take the money out of those belts and put the paper in with a real bill in front so if they check it they will think it's money."

"Where are we going to do all that and not be seen."

"Find an outhouse," she said, looking around the open prairie that had a smattering of military buildings.

"Good idea. There is one behind that building."

"Let's ride over there," she said.

Dismounted, he looked around, seeing several soldiers marching about, others loafing near the stables. She went inside with the two money belts and the cut paper. Flies nosily droned around the raw wood structure, and he stood on one foot, then the other outside.

"Anyone out there?" she asked in a hiss.

"Some scouts, some soldiers is all I see, and they ain't close. You all right in there?"

"It doesn't smell good in here. Give me your blanket roll."

"Sure." He went to his horse, undid it, and then, whistling, came back, and she barely opened the door to take it.

"Whew, that place does stink," he said.

"You should be in here," she said.

"No. I like it out here."

"I have it. Here's your blanket back. The money's inside the roll." He took the roll as she stepped outside and mopped her brow. "Put on the money belt."

"Just one?" he asked, tying his bedroll back on his horse.

"They will know there are two belts. I have on one." She padded her waist.

"I don't like it."

"It is the only way they will think they have the real ones if they rob us."

"I guess you're right. Can we go get married?"

She frowned in disbelief at him. "I smell like an—outhouse."

"Ain't bothering me."

"It is me. Let me take a bath first." She patted his shoulder for him to control his impatience.

They rode back to the cow camp. Shorty felt disappointed. The cowhands planned to ride back with them to Ogallala. Earlier she'd paid them part of their wages, and they had lighted out for town.

"Come with me," Celia said as the sun started to set. With a towel over his arm, Shorty nodded and told Adolph he's see him later. They were almost to the willows up the creek when two masked men stepped out of the brush with pistols.

"I'll take that money," one said, making motions with his fingers.

"You won't get away with this," Shorty said.

"Give me the money or she dies."

"All right, let me get the dang thing off," he said.

"Turn your head for decency sake," she said sharply to the pair.

"Don't try anything."

His fingers fumbled with the shirt buttons, and he undid the buckles. He could see her busy doing the same, and hoped the damn owlhoots weren't looking at her too. At last he drew his money belt out and handed it over.

"Check it," the leader said, handing the belt to the other man.

Shorty held his breath until the second outlaw said, "Money in every pocket and plenty of it." He recognized Moore's voice.

"Thank you, little lady," the leader said, taking hers. "Either of you try anything, I'll shoot her."

"You ain't getting away with this," Shorty threatened.

"That's right," she added.

"You better thank your stars I ain't killing you. Come on, we've got what we want." They backed away and ran off into the cedar brush.

Shorty drew his pistol and fired five quick shots into the brush after the sounds of their fleeing horses.

"What's wrong? What's wrong?" Adolph asked, coming with his sawed-off shotgun ready in his hands. "I heard shots."

"We been robbed." She laughed. "Robbed of all our newspapers."

"What does that mean?" Adolph frowned at them.

"Means they didn't get her money," Shorty punched new cartridges in his revolver. Celia came over and swung on his arm.

"That's good." Adolph laughed too.

25

A bright sun shone over the snowy peaks above them. Feather returned from her brisk morning bath in the rushing stream. Slocum gave a shiver as he glanced at her naked copper beauty. Then he turned back to the task of using the single-edge razor on his face. Lathered and softened, the whiskers came clean as he held the edge against them, the keen blade slicing them off at the skin surface.

He rinsed the soap off the blade in the small pan of hot water, and wished for a larger looking glass as he smiled at her. She had dressed, and wore her fringed dress.

"Still got this country to ourselves?" he asked.

"Magpies and blue jays are here."

"I heard them. They've been telling me how to shave."

"Those men, those Ab-b-otts, won't come here?"

"In time they probably will, but we'll be far across the Powder River country by then, I hope."

"What about Bergereon?"

"I'll let the army handle him."

"Good. Then when you finish, we have business in the bedroll before we ride from this place." The mischievous wink in her brown eyes told him enough.

He almost wished they were already over on the Ten Sleep side of the Big Horns. Somewhere in the parks above Ten Sleep Canyon was where the trapper's cabin was that she planned to use. He could almost smell a haunch of mountain sheep roasting in the fireplace. Finished shaving at last, he wiped the blade clean and dried it before he stored it in his things. Then he washed his face in the icy stream, and dried his face on a towel.

How did she dip her body in such cold water? He knew she would be clean and firm from such a bath, waiting for him. What had she said? There was a waterfall above this cabin that was spring-fed and ran all winter. He was anxious to see this place.

He shed his clothes, for he knew under those covers she was naked. At last, with the chill of the sparkling morning on his skin, he dove under the blankets and they quickly sought each other, her cold skin against his warmer body, the muscles and tone of her body sending signals to his brain.

"Hurry," she cried, spreading her hips open under him.

He sought her with an urgency to match his own. Then, when he entered her, he paused at an unfamiliar sound, and both of them listened. Then he raised up on both hands and turned his head to hear—something out there.

"Not ravens?" he asked.

"No, mules," she said with a pale flush under her dark skin.

"Bergereon!" they both said at the same time.

He threw the covers back and jerked her to her feet. They scrambled to dress, their clothes not cooperating. The noise of the pack train grew closer. The hiders were coming right up through their canyon.

His boots on at last, he raced for the horses, and she rolled up their blankets. She came running with her arms loaded and looking back for what she might have missed. He took her armload at the edge of the brush and tossed it from sight behind the boughs of the low-growing evergreens. She rushed back for more.

On foot, he led the horses further up into the side canyon where he hoped their snorts to the mules could not be heard. Out of breath, she joined him and piled their saddles on the ground, then came to help him keep the horses quiet.

"We leave anything?" he asked under his breath.

"Your looking glass," she said in a whisper.

"Hope they miss it."

She nodded sharply in agreement.

He held the Winchester in his hands as he listened to the nearby mule skinners curse and beat on their animals. The clatter of hooves on rocks, jackasses braying, and the men's talking sounded so close that at any moment he expected one of them to come around the pines and discover them.

The horses did not betray them. The noisy mules and cursing hiders went past. The two of them remained in the cover until the hiders were over the high pass and gone from the canyon.

Slocum began to saddle the horses. "They're still in the Black Hills," he said, confused by their presence.

"They probably waited here until they had a place set up to meet Sitting Bull."

"Oh, I see. They stayed out of sight in the mountains until they made contact with Sitting Bull."

"This dog of a man Bergereon is no fool. What will we do next?"

"You need to take word to Lieutenant Schaeffer and tell him where he is," Slocum said, wrestling with himself about their safety and his desire to end Bergereon's days of freedom.

"You want me to ride back to the fort?" she asked.

"That would mean several days there and back," he realized. "No, I'll think of a better plan. Hell, the military and their problems aren't ours. I need to put some distance between me and the Abbott brothers anyway."

"We need to make camp for a few days." She looked at him very seriously. "Otherwise, soon I will bring you bad luck."

He realized her period must be at hand, and he knew how superstitious Indians were about that.

"White men are not afraid of such things," he said. They didn't have time to wait around. Besides, he had none of the misgivings about female body functions that Indian males did.

"Before another blast of winter comes down, let's get to that cabin. We don't need to worry about Bergereon or bad luck," he said to reassure her. It was time they took care of themselves.

Concern clouded her dark eyes, but she agreed with a nod. "I will do as you say."

"Good. It's time to worry about you and me. Let's ride around them and go to the mountains in the west."

"Yes."

The next noontime, they rode out of the last grove of pines and faced a cold north wind that swept their faces on the edge of the sagebrush basin they called Powder River. Seventy to a hundred miles westward lay the Big Horns. He was grateful she knew the streams and places to water, for they entered a trackless land where game trails wandered through the pungent sage. And many miles were left to ride.

"At the mountains, we will need to make snowshoes and must leave our horses behind. Not enough willows up there to feed them all winter." She turned up her blanket to cover her head, and then leaned into the strong breeze sweeping the basin.

"We can do that. I'll be glad when we get there."

The howling wind ravaged at them all day. They made poor time by his calculation. In the late afternoon she led them to a deep coulee with a small spring. He took his telescope and looked over the country. Not a sign of anything. He slipped back to camp and warmed his hands at her small fire where she cooked the haunch of an antelope he had shot earlier.

A few willows around the spring were all that marked the spot in the draw besides the gray sage and brown bunchgrass that carpeted the entire basin. Obviously, from her aloof ways toward him, her period had started that day. She kept herself away from him as much as possible.

"We should cross the Powder River and then ride up Crazy Woman Creek to the foot of the mountains," she said.

"Any danger of riding up on some hostiles?"

"They would be in camp at this time."

"Don't look now," he said. "But we have company."

"Who is it?" she asked.

Someone called out in Sioux, and she rose. "It is a boy I know," she said to Slocum. "He wants to talk is all."

The Indian came downhill on foot. He was hardly more than a youth, but his bowed legs gave him a distinguished gait as he jumped sage and hurried with a rifle in his hand.

"What's he want?" Slocum asked, looking around for more.

She spoke to him in Sioux. He replied and then nodded at Slocum.

"He is a scout for the army," she said.

"Who is his commander?" Slocum asked.

"Schaeffer."

"That sounds more like it. Tell we have information for his lieutenant about Bergereon."

She translated, and the boy said something to her.

"He will bring someone here tomorrow to talk to you."

"Give him some of that antelope to eat."

"You cut it," she said, and stepped back.

Slocum shrugged and stepped in. The boy nodded when Slocum pointed to a portion he intended to cut off for him. With his skinning knife, he sliced off some of the cooked meat, and put it on a tin plate for the scout.

The boy grinned and said something in Sioux.

"He said thank you," she told Slocum.

Slocum nodded and rose with effort to his feet. "Tell him to come anytime and we will share with our friends."

Obviously the army had not found Bergereon's train. They had their work cut out for them. After the boy finished eating, his dark lips slick with grease, he spoke to her, and then he nodded in appreciation at Slocum. In a flash, he was gone over the hill, and only the wind overhead kept them company in their camp.

After eating, Slocum climbed the rise and made an inspection in the sharp wind of the vast basin. There was nothing obvious, but he reminded himself that he had not seen the scout approaching either. He returned to camp as the sun settled in the west, and reassured her that he'd seen nothing out of place. They took separate bedrolls and turned in.

During the night he awoke to listen to wolves prowling the basin. Their howling soon signaled they were moving away, and he set the Colt down under the covers and went back to sleep.

They stayed in camp the next morning. The wind abated some, and the temperatures climbed. He reset a shoe on a small bay that she rode.

"The army is coming," she announced, coming down the hillside.

"All of them?" he asked, amused.

"Maybe a dozen." She took the small hammer from him when he set the horse's hoof down.

"Good, maybe we can help them find Bergereon."

Schaeffer, a sergeant, three Indian scouts, and a half-dozen troopers came off the sagebrush-choked hillside. The lieutenant reined up and dismounted, handing his reins to a private.

"Slocum, you're a long ways from Nebraska." He pulled off his glove and shook hands, nodding to her.

"You met Feather?" Slocum said.

"Nice to meet you, ma'am." Schaeffer turned back to Slocum. "Where's Bergereon? We've been on a wild-goose chase and haven't seen a sign of him."

"He came out of the Black Hills just ahead of us. Feather figures he's got an appointment with the old man, Sitting Bull, somewhere."

"How long ago did you see him?" Schaeffer looked concerned.

"Two days. He was in the heart of the hills."

"That's why we haven't found any sign. He's been behind us and not ahead of us."

"That's it. He almost rode into our camp."

"You never saw any more of him?"

"Frankly, with only me and her, I swung south to avoid him."

"That makes sense."

"He's either passed you or is about to."

"That's the best news I've had in days. I need to get him before he delivers those rifles." Schaeffer had a grim set to his jaw.

"He still had them when he passed us, I'd say," Slocum

told him. "Or he had lots of empty mules they were pushing hard over the grade."

"None of my business, but where are you headed?" Schaeffer asked.

"A place to winter up."

Schaeffer closed his eyes, shook his head, and then drew in a deep breath. "I'm jealous as hell." A wide grin covered his face as he stuck out his hand. "Have a good winter and I'll see you again, I hope, sometime."

"I'm planning on it," Slocum said. "Good luck getting Bergereon."

"I'll get him thanks to you. Ma'am, thanks for your help too," he said to her, and then went to his horse.

In the saddle, Schaeffer saluted them, and then told the sergeant they were moving out. Several of the troopers waved at Slocum, and they all reined their mounts around and rode up the slope in cat-hops. On the top Schaeffer waved again, and they were gone.

"Let's get saddled," Slocum said to her. "We need to make the Powder River by dark."

Feather smiled at him, and it warmed him.

26

The second day, they reached where Crazy Woman Creek spilled out of the Big Horns, and he pulled the shoes off the horses to turn them loose. There was plenty of grazing at the lower elevations, and he wondered if the Texas ponies would still be around the area when springtime arrived. If not, he'd find some more. Feather discovered a large hollow fallen tree to stash their saddles and blankets inside. With a hand ax, he shaped a plug to block the end and save their tack from the salt-hungry teeth of varmints over the winter. Their gear stored, she steamed and bent willow stalks into snowshoes. They made a backpack apiece to carry their things from the deer and antelope hides she had saved.

"Wait," she said when he was ready at last to pick up his pack and start out.

From her things she pulled out a pair of new moccasins for him.

"These will be better than your boots."

He shook his head, impressed with how she had made him a pair of moccasins and he had not known about it. He sat down on a log and removed his left boot. Grateful, he pulled on the first moccasins, and nodded in approval at the fit. Then he pulled on the next one, as she stowed his boots in his backpack.

"I owe you," he said, and stepped around in his new comfortable footgear. "We better get to hiking."

She nodded her approval.

Soon, with his rifle in hand and bedrolls and packs on their backs, they took the trail up the deep narrow canyon.

Feather had mentioned that it would require perhaps three days to reach the park. The Crazy Woman Creek trail was narrow and steep; in places they brushed boughs and bluff walls, but managed to squeeze through. Slocum regretted not having taken their horses, but he knew they would have had to be destroyed once they reached the park because there was nothing to graze.

They came out in the snow once they reached the top of the canyon and the divide lay ahead of them, so they camped for the night. He saw three moose in the willows on the creek, but didn't bother to kill one of them because he and Feather were too far from their winter camp to save the meat.

"There will be more," she said to reassure him, and put her hand on his arm.

It was the first time that she had touched him in two days. Perhaps her period was about over, or else she was learning his ways. No matter. He stretched the tired muscles of his back. The real test was ahead. He hoped that a snow storm didn't catch them short of their destination. Clouds were floating through the peaks above them.

They started out with their loaded backpacks for the pass before dawn, and they found the snow dry and shallow enough that there was no need for snowshoes. Through the lodgepole-pine forest they crossed the wide level bench, until again the grade shifted upward and the steep gray-granite peaks fanned out before them.

The temperatures were colder, and he was grateful for the mittens she'd made. Late that afternoon, they built a lean-to under the timberline to reflect the campfire's heat on them.

She cooked more of the antelope and they melted snow for coffee.

It began to snow before dark, and the thick white petals fell around them and disappeared in the orange flames as they sat cross-legged, enjoying their meal and the fire's company.

"Tomorrow we go over the divide," she promised. "Then one more day and we will be there."

He agreed, busy eating his food. Their antelope meat would soon be used up. Walking ten-plus miles a day in the cold required lots of energy. He would need to kill something soon to supply them with adequate food. There would be few things to hunt this high up. The small headache pounding at his forehead and his shortness of breath told him they were at a high altitude.

She leaned over and put her face on his shoulder. "Was I wrong to bring you up here?"

"No. I am anxious to reach the cabin."

"So am I." She sat up, obviously also weary from the day's hiking.

At mid-morning the next day there were flurries as they crossed the hard windswept pass and a great snowy basin appeared before them. Between blasts of flakes, he could see the western slopes of the Big Horns spread out beneath them. They had gone through the pass. He kissed her, and then smiled despite his cracked lips.

"Let's go," he said above the howling wind, and they started down the white slope.

They had reached the level ground when the flat report of a rifle slapped the dry snow and he whirled in time to see the shooter high above them. Bergereon was in the pass on a mule. Slocum shoved her down.

"Take cover," he said, and drew the rifle to his shoulder.

"Damn you, Slocum!" Bergereon roared, and tried to fight his circling mule and reload his sharps. "I'll get you this time!"

The distance was too far, but Slocum took aim anyway. His rifle's report hurt his ears, and he levered in another shell. His vision blurred by the cutting wind, he squeezed off another shot. This one found its mark. Hit hard, Bergereon threw his rifle in the air and fell from the mule. The jackass began to plunge down the mountainside.

"I've got him!" she shouted, and started uphill to catch the mule.

Slocum nodded grimly. "Be careful! Bergereon may only be wounded!"

She plowed through the snow to head the mule off. He could hear her voice above the wind speaking to the wide-eyed riderless animal. Slocum began the climb back up the steep face of the mountain. How had Bergereon gotten there?

Obviously the buffalo hunter had ridden up their backtrail. Were there any others with him? Randolph—wasn't that his henchman's name? The cold thin air sliced at Slocum's throat as he fought unsteady footing in the frozen mountainside. He gasped for air, until at last he looked down at Bergereon's still form. He was on his back, and his steel-blue eyes never flicked. Blood had soaked out of a dark hole in his coat from the wound in his chest.

"You should have gone to Canada," Slocum said aloud, and satisfied the man was dead or close to it, he turned in his tracks and started for the flat far below where Feather held the mule. If there were more of them, he'd handle them too.

At the base of the mountain he hugged her.

"Is he dead?" she asked, casting a glance up the slope.

"If he ain't, he soon will be," he said.

"Were there others?"

"I didn't have the energy to go back over the top and look," he said. "Beside's with the snow blowing, wouldn't see much."

"What if there are more?" she asked, huddling under her blanket.

"Then they better have funeral suit's ready. Let's get out of here." He cast a long look back at the pass above them. The flying flakes obscured the dark figure lying on the mountainside for a moment. Then he saw it, and felt satisfied that Bergereon would rest there forever. If there were others coming after him, they'd better come ready to die.

They loaded their packs on the mule and headed westward. Snow squalls increased, and they were forced to wade through deeper snow. At dark they reached the headwaters of Ten Sleep Creek, and found some willows for the famished mule to eat.

Slocum built a small lean-to, and she cooked the last quarter of the antelope. They had some jerky in reserve, but he would need to get some meat in the next twenty-four hours or the pickings in their camp would be thin.

He warmed by the fire and considered the day. Bergereon was dead up on the pass. The few minutes of the encounter passed before him like a great mural, and he considered them both lucky. They had not been completely safe ever since they'd left Ft. Robinson. She settled down beside him and hugged him.

"Your medicine is strong. At first I thought I had cursed you, but I hadn't."

"No, you are good medicine," he said, and patted her hand on his shoulder.

27

They slogged the last half mile up the canyon on snowshoes. The mule floundered and fought his way in the drifts, with Feather pushing and Slocum pulling on his lead.

"It is at the head of this draw," she announced, out of breath.

He nodded. Catching his breath, he studied the aspens and the lodgepole pines on the steep slopes that lined the wide trough of a park filled with knee-deep snow. They were close, and that was all that mattered. Later, he would have to slip off the mountains to the west and release the mule. Feather thought there were enough willows nearby to feed him for a while at the cabin.

"Ready?" she asked when he finished flexing his back.

"Yes."

"Gittup!" she shouted at the mule, and slapped him on the butt with her hand. When the mule started to walk in Slocum's prints, he turned with the rope over his shoulder and resumed their drive up the valley.

Then he saw the dark log walls of the cabin under a heavy load of snow. It was there, just as she'd promised.

"That's it!" she shouted, and fought her way past the mule. "What's wrong?" she asked with a frown as Slocum hurried past her.

"Supper," he said, and drew the rifle from the mule. He

looked close for another telltale flicker of ears in the shaded timber. Then he made out the moose yearling standing perfectly still looking at them from the timber at the base of the slope.

The rifle barked and the half-grown moose stumbled to his knees. Slocum reloaded and waited, ready to shoot him again, but the yearling fell over on his side. They hugged each other and danced in the knee-deep powder.

"There's enough meat to last us," he shouted.

"Yes, and tender too."

"Right. Let's go run those packrats out of that shack," he said, and then he kissed her. "Then we'll butcher him."

In mid-afternoon, Shorty drove the chuck wagon, and his bride Celia shared the spring seat. They were going home. Adolph rode with the boys and helped drive the remuda. That way the newlyweds had the days to themselves.

"Reckon we can hide that money somewhere in the wagon tonight?" he asked.

"Why?" Celia asked, crowded close to him and hugging his right arm.

"It's getting lumpy to sleep on."

She laughed, and then she kissed him on the cheek. "Do you think that Slocum got away from those bounty hunters?"

"I hadn't thought of him in days." Shorty considered it for a long time, and then he nodded to dismiss her concerns. "They never got him."

Strange thing. He hadn't noticed the weather or much of anything else but her since they were married by the chaplain at the fort. The weather had turned colder, he decided, and turned up his collar.

"You cold?" she asked, sounding concerned, and reached in the back for a blanket. Soon she had the wrap over him and tucked in. "That better, dear?"

"Fine. Someone's coming," he said, studying the prairie.

"I can see it. Not Indians."

"No. It's not Indians. Looks more like a buckboard."

"I think it's Bruce," she said in a small voice.

"That day was coming too," Shorty said, and began to whistle "Oh, Susanna."

"You won't shoot him?"

"I'll try not to," he said.

"Oh, Shorty, I don't know what I'd do if—" She chewed on her lip as the rig drew closer.

At last, they drew abreast. His right arm in a sling, Bruce blinked at first at her, then at Shorty.

"Got some news for you," Shorty announced. "Me and your sister are man and wife. Sorry you missed the festivities, but we decided you were too broke up to dance anyway."

"Married . . ." Bruce acted thunderstruck. His leg was still in a cast, and his pale face soon matched the bandage.

"Yes, and we want you to know we plan to be partners in the ranch with you."

"Partners?"

"You having trouble hearing me?" Shorty frowned at the man, and Celia squeezed his arm hard. He glanced over, and saw her frown in disapproval.

"The cattle sold well, fifteen cents a pound," she announced.

"A pound?" Bruce asked.

"It's been some drive," Shorty said, wondering about his brother-in-law's hearing. "We're going about another few miles and bed down for the night. We can talk about it then in camp."

"Oh, yes," Bruce said, still apparently in shock.

Shorty clucked to the mules, and she held a death grip on his arm.

"I think he took it all right," she said, sounding worried.

"How else could he take it?"

"Shorty, you don't need to inflame him."

"He better get used to his two partners. His days being the king are over at the MC Ranch."

"Oh, heavens," she said, and looked to the cloudy sky for help.

Shorty set the mules into a trot. The first set-to with Bruce was over, and it hadn't gone half bad. There would be worse ones. Maybe he should tell Bruce privately that he could find himself a woman of his own at that hog ranch. Then he chuckled to himself.

"What's so funny?"

"Nothing, darling. I was wondering where Slocum's camping tonight."

"No telling."

"I'll bet he's up in the high country where the snow's deep as this wagon top."

"You think so?"

Shorty laid the rein to the lazy wheel mule and laughed. "Buried in the snow, I'd bet, with that Injun woman Feather." Then he laughed aloud, and she shook his arm and made a face of disapproval.

"Army's coming," Barley Burns shouted to Shorty as they stopped work at the forge in the new shop on the MC Ranch. They'd been all morning making a new piece for the mower machine that they were rebuilding. Wouldn't be long before spring, and they'd need to put up lots of hay. Bruce and the mules had wrecked the mower the summer before. Shorty intended to have it operating before the spring thaw.

A nice open March day welcomed them when they stepped outside. Shorty recognized Lieutenant Shaeffer and his men in their buffalo coats. They looked road-weary, and the tattered yellow guidon flapped in the wind.

"Hello, Shorty."

"Howdy, Lieutenant. This is Barley Burns, my right-hand man."

"Good to see you, young man." The officer dismounted.

"Guess you're coming back from Powder River? You seen Slocum lately?" Shorty asked as he stood outside the shop, holding the suspenders of his leather apron.

"Not since last fall. Him and the Sioux woman were headed for the Big Horns. He put us on Bergereon's trail, and we managed to stop them from selling those rifles to Sitting Bull. We captured his pack train and his men, but Bergereon and his partner Randolph got away. We trailed them to the foot of the Big Horns, but lost them in a snowstorm."

"Did Bergereon and Randolph get into the Big Horns?"

Shorty asked, feeling sick to his stomach at the notion.

"Yeah, but someone answering Bergereon's description was found dead up in the pass by a renegade."

"You think it was him?"

"Yes, I do. The Indian said he'd been shot once in the chest, and the buck took some personal things from the body that my men thought belonged to Bergereon. A letter in written in French from Canada too."

"Sounds like him. What about Randolph?"

"I'm not sure about him. He may be hiding up there with a few renegade Cheyenne bucks somewhere over the pass on the Ten Sleep side. No way to get up there until it thaws, except go to Montana and come down the Bridger trace. Why do you ask?"

"Just wondered. I appreciate your stopping by. I'm glad someone got Bergereon. Maybe the same thing will happen to Randolph."

"Maybe. There are warrants out for him if he shows up."

"Good. Guess you'll be glad to get back to Ft. Cottonwood?"

"Yes, but I have to report next to Ft. Lincoln and join Colonel Custer's Seventh. Sherman wants all the hostiles gathered up and placed on reservations this coming summer."

"Good luck at that." Shorty had a grim set to his mouth. Tonight, he could tell Celia that the man she hated so was dead at last; that would be enough. He wouldn't mention that Randolph was still on the loose. "Thanks for stopping by. That was good news."

Shaeffer saluted them, and then rode off with his men.

"You figure that Slocum shot him?" Barley asked as the troopers rode out the gate.

"He sure did it if Bergereon gave him the chance."

"What's eating you, Shorty?" Barley asked.

"I figure Slocum still might have another one to get." Shorty wondered how his old partner was doing. But there was no way he could go help him.

Slocum stood in the timber and studied the smoldering logs of the cabin. His heart was so heavy, he thought it would bust. Feather—where was she? He had seen the smoke from far away, and known when he set out there would be trouble at their place. At first he'd expected that the fireplace had set the cabin on fire. Luckily, he had slipped in and gone around, or he might have run smack into the band of blanket-ass cutthroats that had waded through the snow and gone to the west only a short while ago loaded down with loot. He'd counted six of them. One of them had been a white man or a breed, but at the distance Slocum had not been able to tell which.

He closed his eyes. Best he go down there and find her. He angled down the hill in the last light of the day. In the snow he found her still form face-down, and he rushed to kneel beside her. The snow was red with her blood from the scalping. He turned her over, and knew life had left her body.

"Damn you killers," he swore, and closed his eyes.

With a heavy heart, he wrapped her body, then put it on a platform amid some lodgepoles in the way of her people. Long past dark he used starlight to track the attackers back to their lair. He sat on a rock ledge and studied the camp below. They were all getting drunk on firewater, dancing and war-whooping. He undid the one blanket on his backpack and wrapped himself against the cold to wait until they slept.

His eyes dry from the cold wind, he rose to his feet when the last dancer staggered into his tepee. In the camp, Slocum doubled-loaded all the muzzle-loading rifles, using all the extra powder that he could find. He took a rock to batter the hammers of two repeaters. With single-shot buffalo gun, he drove two pieces of lead down the barrel and far enough inside that they were unseen. Then he began to pile brush and boughs around the outside of the three tepees.

Once a grunting Indian rose, came outside, looked around in a drunken haze, pissed, and went back to sleep. Slocum crouched on his heels until satisfied that the man was deep asleep again. Then he took their winter-thin ponies and led them to the bluff above the camp. Then he came back and found two kegs of white lightning. With the raw whiskey, he soaked his tinder as well as the hide sides of the tepees.

He began striking lucifers and lighting his piles of tinder. Flames began to lap up. Satisfied the whole camp would be an inferno shortly, he hurried to the bluff as the cold sun began to dawn.

Flames licked up at the sides of tepees when bucks inside began to cough. Someone screamed and started out an entrance, but a well-placed bullet beside him made him shout and draw back inside. With each entrance facing the sun and the sun over his back, Slocum had the edge. The infernos grew greater, and naked bucks used their knives to cut their way out the backs of the tepees. Half naked or with only a blanket to cover themselves, they tried to fire at this devil on the mountain with his deadly rifle pinning them down.

Rifles exploded, maiming their owners who fell on the snow crying in blinded pain. The tepee walls were so much aflame by this time that he knew they would be destroyed by the fire. No weapons, no shelter, no clothing—the Indians would be hard-pressed to survive.

"That you, Slocum?" someone called as he came through the smoke.

"Yes, it is me. Up here, Randolph," Slocum shouted.

"You better have your prayers said," the man called, and raised the Sharps rifle to his shoulder.

Slocum stood up to make a better target for him. The embattled Indians began to mumble to each other, to point and look at him. *What sort of a fool would stand exposed for a man to shoot at him with a 50-caliber buffalo gun? This white man must have strong medicine.*

Randolph sighted down the sights, and then he squeezed the trigger. The confident look exploded when the rifle blew up. The Cheyennes had had enough. Screaming, they fled into the snowy trees for their lives, afraid that this godlike avenger had great powers and that he would do the same to them that he did to the buffalo hunter.

Slocum turned and mounted the best Cheyenne horse. He took the others along on a lead. They were weak, and he hoped that lower down in the Ten Sleep Canyon there was some willow bark left for them to eat. With the stench of burning hides in his nose, he looked to the blue sky and hoped that Feather had seen his revenge and was pleased. More than anything else, he hoped that she was pleased.